Also by Stone Cruz
From Indigo Sea Press

Back in the Saddle

Pet, the Teacher

indigoseapress.com

The Concierge Apprentice

By

Stone Cruz

Bramble Patch Books
Published by Indigo Sea Press
Winston-Salem

Bramble Patch Books
Indigo Sea Press
PO Box 26701
Winston-Salem, NC 27114

First Bramble Patch Books edition published
March, 2017
Bramble Patch Books, Moon Sailor and all production design are trademarks of Indigo Sea Press, used under license.

For information regarding bulk purchases of this book, digital purchase and special discounts, please contact the publisher at indigoseapress@gmail.com

Cover design by Pan Morelli
Manufactured in the United States of America
ISBN 978-1-63066-466-4

For the concierge everywhere,
and the guests so well served.

Chapter One

Jasper felt his mouth drop open as he stopped in front of the hotel. He stood on the sidewalk, stunned and motionless, then let go of the handle of his rolling suitcase as he pulled the brochure from his shirt pocket.

"This can't be right," he muttered.

The photo on the flyer he held showed the name of the hotel—*Hotela Plus De Plaisir*—in brilliant, fire-engine red, six-inch script letters against a bright gold background. He lifted his eyes toward the dull coral on faded yellow. He leaned back, looking from left to right, taking in the entire weathered front of the establishment. Much as he wanted to believe had had arrived at the wrong address, there was no denying he was standing before the hotel where he was supposed to work through the summer.

"The hurricane?" he asked absently. "Do you suppose this was all under water and they just never fixed up the front?" The interior, he promised himself, would be in good repair.

Pushing his way through the glass front door—pausing to lift the rollers on his suitcase from where it hooked the loose edge of the worn carpet—Jasper stopped. He gazed around the foyer of the hotel, wrestling with whether or not he should simply return to the airport and try to get a flight back from New Orleans to Idaho.

The furniture and decorations appeared to be an aged version of the accoutrements pictured on the back of the brochure. Then he realized these were actually the very same furnishings and appointments. And they were sitting in the identical spots around the large, open space. Only everything was much, much—in fact decades—older than it had been when the picture was made. The cushions on the sofas were flattened with use. The upholstery of the chairs was frayed to varying degrees. The wooden legs of the tables were chipped. The entire scene had a look of weary obsolescence to it.

When had this style been in vogue, Jasper asked himself. When he first saw the illustrated brochure, he had assumed the decor of the hotel was designed to be an intentional throwback to the modernist, contemporary style of the late 50s or early 60s. He

1

realized, as the flood of despair rose up within him, that the photos were the originals taken sixty years before he got to New Orleans and that the hotel had not been updated—or even rearranged—since then.

The dusty silence was broken by a snort, quickly followed by an outright, uninhibited snore. Jasper walked toward the check-in desk. Sleeping in an office chair, his feet propped on the counter, was an unshaven, balding, round little man. Jasper judged him to be in his late forties, or maybe fifties.

Quietly he consulted the brochure again. "Nope," he whispered. "At least he wasn't sleeping here back then."

He cleared his throat. And when the man did not respond, he spoke. "Excuse me."

The sleeper jumped, pulling his feet off the counter. "Not yet," he said, struggling to wake up. "Check in time is not until 2 p.m."

Jasper drew a deep breath. "I'm supposed to talk to Mr. Sol Simon."

The man behind the counter tilted his head and closed on eye. "Who did you say you are?" He studied the tall, lean, tousle-haired young man before him warily.

"Jasper Merritt. From Idaho Tech. The hospitality concierge apprentice program."

"Oh!" The man's face lit with a welcoming smile. "I'm Mr. Simon. And you're Merritt, eh? Our new night manager."

"Night? Night manager? No," he protested. "I'm supposed to be a concierge. I'm the concierge apprentice."

"Concierge. Night manager." Sol shrugged as he got to his feet. "We wear a lot of hats around here." He grasped Jasper's hand. "I'm sure glad to see you, son. Welcome to the *Hotela Plus De Plaisir*."

"*Hotela Plus*—so that's how you pronounce—"

"It's French. *Plus De Plaisir*. Lots of things are French around here. It translates 'Hotel of High Pleasure.'"

Jasper felt his jaw drop again. "Hotel of Pleasure? This isn't—"

"No, no, no. New Orleans has plenty of cat houses and sex shops, but this ain't one. No." he picked up a walkie-talkie. "We're a legit place of lodging." He keyed the radio and spoke into it. "Flo, please come to the lobby right away, darlin'."

Sol spoke with the odd Louisiana accent Jasper had noticed half a dozen times since he got off the plane at Louis Armstrong Airport.

It almost sounded like a slower, prettier New York City accent. "That's not to say ain't a lot of sex goes on around here. There's a gracious plenty." He winked at Jasper. "And we don't pay no attention to who checks in with who or how long they stay. If you know what I mean." He bumped Jasper with his shoulder. "Maybe they don't teach you that at the university. But that's the first lesson of real-world hospitality."

"Well, as a concierge, I understand—"

Sol keyed the mic again. "Flo, sweetheart, I mean right now."

A brief burst of static came over the radio, followed by the voice of a young woman. "I hear you first time, Sol. Don't take your shirt off."

The female voice was accented very differently than Sol's. It was, Jasper realized, a Cajun accent.

Sol laughed. "She means, 'Keep your shirt on.' Tizzy's going to be so glad you're here."

"Tizzy?"

"Yeah. She's been working the nights and I been doing the days. You don't never get to spend time together that way. I said to her, 'Just wait until this Merritt fellow gets here. I'm take you to Kenner to see the ponies, my love. They running now. You like horse racing, Jasper?"

"Uh. I've never been."

"Well you have to go, you know. What do you all do for fun in Idaho besides count potatoes?"

"Count— Listen, Mr. Simon, I just got here. Things aren't quite the way I was led to believe they would be. I have a lot of questions."

"I know. I know," Sol said in a consoling tone. "That's why I called Flo to come down. She explain everything to you. She can answer all your questions."

"Is she the executive administrator?"

"No. She the housekeeper."

"The house—"

"But she knows everything. She set up our computer reservations, our new finance ledger. She do the ordering. Flo pretty much knows everything."

For the second time in five minutes Jasper started to grab his suitcase and take a taxi back to the airport.

3

"Ah, Flo. You here."

He turned, more to leave than to see whom Sol was addressing, and stared straight over the head of the person standing beside him. Instantly his gaze dropped to the hazel, intense eyes of the twenty-year-old woman who stared back at him. She was, he realized as he took her in, pretty and intriguing in ways he had never experienced. She stood, hands-on-hips, studying him as he looked at her. A splash of freckles adorned the bridge of her nose, almost in comic counterpoint to the inquisitive fierceness of her gaze. Her face was shaped like a heart and crowned with light brown hair only a few shades darker than his. Beneath her open, long-sleeved white shirt she wore a stretch halter top over her round, ample breasts. The curves below were unconcealed by her well-worn, tight blue jeans. And suddenly Jasper recognized he wasn't in such a rush to go back to the airport.

"Hmph." She made a dismissive sound and tilted her head. "So you Merritt, the long-awaited manager of the night."

"Manager? I'm—I'm—" he stuttered. "I'm supposed to be the concierge in training. A concierge is—"

"I know what that is," she cut him off abruptly. "Concierge be French. You think I don't know the French?"

"Well—" he stammered, "I am supposed to be in training. I'm supposed to be the apprentice concierge."

He felt Sol grasp the back of his elbow.

"Flo, you take my boy here and give him the grand tour." He pushed Jasper toward the girl. "Make sure to answer all his questions what you can. Just make sure he ready to go on tonight at 8 p.m."

Jasper turned to him. "Eight? I have to run the desk by myself tonight by 8 p.m.?"

"Eight tonight until 8 in the morning. It's Monday, son. Things be slow. Nothing to it," Sol said expansively. "And you need help, you just call Manuel on the walkie-talkie."

"Manuel?"

"Come on, boy." The girl had grasped his wrist as if he were a child who wasn't where he was supposed to be. "First you see your room and get rid, of your bags."

Jasper was filled with reluctance. Should he resist this instant indoctrination, filled with assumptions about him, and refuse to go

4

where the girl wanted to lead him? Going along with her, he thought, was a signal that he was accepting—even complicit—with this whole, crazy misrepresentation of what he was supposed to be doing.

"You not afraid of elevators?"

"No," he replied. "Of course not."

"That's 'cause you never ride in our elevator." She snickered as the door rolled shut and the elevator began to rise.

"Your room on third floor. Room 312."

Jasper stood silently trying to grasp his situation. "This is all wrong." He shook his head. "The hotel isn't what it's supposed to be. Being the desk clerk is not what I'm supposed to do. I feel like I'm being railroaded. Surely the people at the university had no idea this was going to happen."

The housekeeper seemed to be sizing him up. She showed no concern whatever about his anxiety. The faintest smile played across her eyes and lips.

"Where you from, boy?"

"My name is Jasper Merritt."

"What a mouthful. You 'Jaz' now."

"Excuse me?"

"You Jaz. That's you Nola name." The door rolled open and she grabbed his wrist again and pulled him down the hallway. "Where you from, Jaz?"

"Idaho," he replied absently, captivated by the disrepair he saw in the hallway. The air was filled with a musty smell and abundant dust motes.

"Where Idaho? Out by California?"

"No. No." He shook his head. "It's in the Northwest. Borders Oregon. And Utah. Nevada. Montana. Wyoming. Canada. . . . I can't believe the hotel actually rents these rooms out to guests."

"No. These rooms not available."

"What?"

"No room for rent above the second floor."

"Seriously? Doesn't this hotel have thirty available rooms?"

"No." She shook her head as they stopped in front of room 312. "We have maybe eighteen, maybe fifteen rooms for rent. Depends on how much other shit Sol have me doing."

He looked back down the hallway toward the elevator. "So

these rooms are not habitable?"

"You don't be worry about these other here rooms, Jaz boy. Just this room." She produced a large, brass key. "Now this here is your key."

He held it before himself, gazing at it as if he never seen a key before. Raising his eyes to hers, he asked, "This hotel doesn't use key cards?"

"That be the master key, Jaz boy. It get you into any room in this hotel." She stood staring at him, hands on hips, waiting expectantly.

He slid the key into the lock and turned it. The heavy wooden door swung open silently and he gazed in. The room was remarkably large and clean. The sheets and bedspread were turned back at one corner, as if a guest were expected. A desk, dresser and several lamps sat neatly around the room.

"Look nice?" the girl asked.

"Very nice. Clean. Neat. Orderly." He glanced down at her. She stood close enough that looking down at her meant seeing her breasts. "You got all this ready for me?"

"Shore. They been waiting on you. I had to make everything good." She took the handle of his suitcase and rolled it to the dresser. "they been so excited for you coming here. You they first apprentice." She motioned toward the desk. "You can put you backpack over there."

"The first apprentice," he echoed. He slid the loops of his pack off his shoulders. "Well, maybe that explains part of this. I don't think they really understood that program when they signed up."

She gave an easy, throaty laugh. "They understand perfect the program, Jaz boy. They needed someone to run the counter and don't have no money for to hire another clerk. Then Sol see this program for college students. He only pay half you money. Some institution pay the rest."

"Yeah. The Hospitality Management Institute," he protested. "But it's supposed to be a training program. Not a summer clerk job." He sat on the edge of the bed. "I'm supposed to learn how to be a concierge. This is to prepare me to step into that role when I graduate next spring."

"Oh, you going to learn plenty, boy." She went to the window and opened the curtains. Brilliant light filled the room. "Now this

6

here looks out on plenty action. We only one block off Bourbon Street. You going to see thing this summer you didn't even know what could happen."

He watched her as she bent over the air conditioner controls and turned the unit on. His eyes were lingering on her perfectly shaped bottom when she glanced back at him, and he looked away.

"Well," he said thoughtfully, "I'm sympathetic with Sol's wanting to spend time with his wife."

"His wife?"

"Yeah. His wife. What's her name? Dizzy?"

She laughed again. "Oh, you mean Tizzy. Tizzy ain't his wife."

"Oh. I just thought— I mean, I thought he was married."

"Sol married for sure." She stood in front of him, hands on hips. "But Tizzy ain't his wife. She just his girl."

". . . Oh."

"Oh yeah."

His head tilted to one side. "Your name is Flo."

"Yeah."

"That's . . ."

"That's what?"

"Well, you are . . . Arcadian, aren't you?"

"Cajun. Say the word. Ain't shamed of what I be."

"Well, okay. It's just, 'Flo' seems like an odd name for a Cajun girl. Is it short for Florence?"

"Look, Jaz boy, my name is Fleur. Fleur Printemps. They can't say that 'round here. So they call me Flo."

"Fleur . . ."

"Fleur Printemps. In English it translates 'Spring Flower.'"

"That's pretty. It suits you."

She tightened her hands on her hips, the feisty, independent expression returning to her face. "Now here the next thing for you to learn, Jaz boy. Maybe most important thing. Will keep you from having a bad summer in total."

". . . Yeah?"

"I got a boyfriend."

"Yeah?"

"He be Anton." She tilted her head to the side. "Now Anton, he maybe not quite as tall as you, but his arms—the size of your legs."

"Oh. . . . I see."

7

"And Anton. He can say my name proper. He know everything I like. And I know how to make him smile." She drew out the word "smile" and smiled broadly as she did. "He something of the jealous kind. Anton say, he don't want nobody close enough to smell his spring flower."

"I see. And why are you telling me this?"

She smirked. "I seen you, boy. You check out my upstairs. You check out my downstairs."

"Uh." He stopped himself from saying it was impossible not to focus on her picturesque breasts or her perfectly etched behind. "I hope you understand that my comment about your name was simply an innocuous compliment. I meant nothing sexual by it. My interest is to be solely profession in all my relationships. Especially with hotel staff."

She studied him. "What is that word? Nock-you-us?"

"Innocuous," he said, and continued cynically. "It's English for 'harmless.'"

"Um hmm. Okay." She pointed toward the restroom. "well you bound to need to pee and then put away your stuff. When you get ready, come down to the lobby and I'll show you everything you need to know for tonight."

He sighed. "Right."

She walked silently from the room, closing the door behind her.

Jasper shook his head. "How am I supposed to be around her for ten weeks and not pay attention to her? Guess, every time I get horny, I'll just think of Anton. That'll put the fear of God in me." He gazed about himself. "So what am I going to do? This is not at all what I signed up for. This has nothing to do with being a concierge."

He got up and opened the zipper pouch on his backpack that held his smart phone. Activating the contact list, he found the number he wanted and called it. Almost instantly a familiar voice answered.

"Deke Hanover."

"Oh, Dr. Hanover! I'm so glad you're in your office. This is Jasper Merritt."

"Hello, Mr. Merritt." The voice was distracted and slow. "How are things in New Orleans?"

"Hot and sticky, sir."

"Wait 'til August. You haven't felt hot and sticky yet."

"Yes, sir. Sir, there's a problem here."

"Oh?" Hanover's tone was casual.

"Sir, this hotel is nothing like the brochure or the information. Once upon a time it might have been a premier hospitality establishment, but it's pretty much a dump now."

"Do tell?" Hanover sounded completely unconcerned.

"Sir, the photo in that brochure is apparently forty or fifty—or sixty—years-old. And every piece of furniture, every accessory in the lobby is not only the same as in the photos—they haven't even been rearranged."

"Hmm," he responded slowly, "so the hotel is like that Miss Havisham in *Great Expectation*: ancient, but still wearing her wedding dress and sitting in the midst of her decorations."

Jasper thought about it. "Well, yes, sir, but I'm pretty sure there's no virginity or innocence around here. The manager lied about everything in the information packet. They may have thirty rooms, but only fifteen are in service."

"I see."

"And the worst of it is that they have no concierge program. When I showed up, they started calling me the 'night manager' right away. One of the housekeepers told me they applied for the hospitality program so they could hire me at half price."

". . . That is a shame, Mr. Merritt."

"A shame? Dr. Hanover, we have to do something. This whole *Hotela Plus De Plaisir* is a sham. It's a fraud. It's a relic."

"Uh huh. What do you suggest we do, Mr. Merritt?"

"Well . . . this isn't a concierge program. I signed up to be part of a concierge program. Can I get into a real hospitality establishment with a legitimate program?"

The professor sighed. "Mr. Merritt, I understand your disappointment. I truly do. But all the assignments have been given out. I have no alternative place to send you. Plus, the Pleasure Hotel—"

"Oh my god. You knew what it meant?"

"You can't get a doctorate without learning French, Mr. Merritt. As I was saying, the hotel has paid its part of your stipend. I'm afraid you're stuck, son."

There was silence between them for a time.

Finally, quietly, Jasper spoke. "I really wanted to learn to be a concierge, Dr. Hanover."

"Well, you will learn a great deal, Jasper. That's your nature. And on your credentials, as far as the world is concerned, you will have been trained to be a concierge."

". . . Yes, sir."

"Enjoy, Mr. Merritt. I'm sure in New Orleans there will be many things to distract you from your plight."

"Right. I'm only one block away from Bourbon Street, sir."

"Goodbye." The phone went dead.

Slowly Jasper lay back on the bed and dropped the phone beside him. "I am stuck all right. Thanks for nothing, doc." He shook his head. "What the hell am I going to do?"

Lying on his back, weary and defeated, staring at the ancient plaster ceiling, he did not even feel himself drifting off to sleep. An hour later he woke with a start, disoriented. In a moment he remembered where he was and why he felt such despair.

Options ran through his mind. He could forego the summer internship altogether. What impact would it have on his graduation? Most likely he would not graduate with his class. He would have to go through an actual concierge apprenticeship program the following summer—and Hanover, his mentor, would not be pleased.

He sighed.

Following through with ten weeks at the Pleasure Hotel would be much simpler. All he had to be was the night clerk. The thought of it made him feel like a fraud.

Jasper stood. He put away his clothes. He washed his face and put on a nice shirt and a tie. Drawing a deep breath, he left the room, rode the elevator down and went to the lobby.

Flo, standing beside Sol, glanced up at him and grinned broadly. "Look here at you, Jaz. You look sharp, boy."

"Thanks," he said tersely, hands in his pockets.

"Here be your name tag." She handed him a thick, plastic tag. "You the concierge."

He held it before him, reading the inscription. The top line was a single word, "Jaz," with a line in smaller text below it, "Concierge Apprentice."

Jasper shook his head. "Jaz isn't my name."

"Can you work the engraving machine?" she asked.

"No."

She shrugged. "I guess your name be Jaz."

10

Chapter Two

From the moment she entered the lobby and walked toward the check in, the woman exuded confidence, elegance and class. Using his recently perfected ability to watch someone without appearing to stare, Jasper admired her as she approached him.

Her slate gray purse and shoes perfectly matched the short-sleeved dress that fit her form closely without being tight. Over one shoulder was the strap of a bag that might have been a valise full of business documents, or it might have been an overnight bag containing the clothes she would wear tomorrow. She was, he guessed, in her mid-40s—or even a bit older—and fairly tall, perhaps 5'8" or 5'9". Her skin was flawless and her shoulder length auburn hair was cut straight and parted on one side. Jasper assumed she was a professional or an executive. She was a remarkably lovely woman.

Why was she at the Pleasure Hotel? Probably, he thought, she had been fooled by the same brochure he had seen. Or even more likely, she had been on the website, where the very same ancient photos had been posted to trick potential guests. He wondered if she would suddenly become aware that she had walked into a dump, then turn and walk right back out the door.

As she stopped before him and he lifted his eyes to hers, he caught the slightest scent of a powdery perfume. She was, he realized, elegant in every way.

She smiled. "You're new."

No. Since she had obviously been to the hotel before, her being there was no mistake. His back-up assumption, then, was that she was there to meet someone discretely.

"How are you, ma'am? Welcome to the *Hotela Plaisir*. How may I help you?"

She had a bright, very pleasing smile. "I believe I have a reservation. The name is 'L. Smith.'"

Smith? Yes, she was definitely at the Pleasure Hotel for confidential purposes.

He found her card instantly in the reservation bin. The only lines filled in were her name and the room she had been assigned: "L.

Smith. Room 204." She was, he surmised, a frequent guest and he knew not to seek any personal information from her.

"Here we are, ma'am. Room 204." He handed her the large, brass key, their fingers brushing. "Would you like to take care of the charge now or when you check out?"

"Now is fine." Her purse snapped open with a muted click and she produced a single $100.

Jasper counted her change quickly and silently and handed it to her as he took the crisp bill. "Would you like a receipt—"

"That won't be necessary." She gazed at him curiously. "So you are a concierge? And your name is Jaz?"

As he put away the money, he heard himself chuckle. It was more emotion than he had intended to display.

"Well, ma'am, my name is actually Jasper." He made eye contact, doing his best to maintain a business-like demeanor. "I am in an international training program for the hospitality industry. Theoretically I'm supposed to be an apprentice concierge." He shrugged. "When the hotel here signed up for the program, I'm not sure they really understood everything it entailed."

She nodded slowly. "They snookered you into a summer job as the night clerk."

He allowed himself a self-conscious laugh. "Well, I think this is a first for the hotel and my co-workers. They take delight in teasing me about being a concierge. And they have decided to call me Jaz."

The woman laughed. "This is New Orleans after all. And that's a perfect name." She glanced toward the front door. "My associate should be coming along any time."

He resisted the urge to say it, and also the urge to laugh when she said it.

"His name is Mr. Jones."

"Yes, ma'am," he replied without emotion. "I'll send him up right away. Should I give him a room key as well?"

"No, no. You don't have to do anything. He knows the room already. I just wanted you to be aware of who this strange man is when he walks through your lobby without saying a word."

"Yes, ma'am."

She hesitated for a second or two, as if there was something else she wanted to ask.

"Ma'am," Jasper said, "if there is anything I can do to make your stay more enjoyable, please do not hesitate to let me know."

Nodding, she responded, "Okay then," and went to the elevator. As she waited, she turned back toward Jasper and smiled at him. Then she entered the elevator and disappeared.

Immediately he began to watch for the mysterious Mr. Jones. What kind of man, he wondered, would be having a clandestine encounter with this classy woman? Jasper pictured someone older than the woman, probably wealthy and important. Maybe someone who, in some community, was well known, which was why they chose to meet in a decrepit, "expired" hotel like this.

Or perhaps Mr. Jones was not at all from Ms. Smith's social class. Maybe he was a beefy, virile working man. Or someone half her age. One thing was sure, Jasper would make no eye contact with him. He would not acknowledge or look in the direction of Mr. Jones, unless the secret lover first spoke to him.

As the minutes passed, Mr. Jones did not arrive. Two parties did come through the front door. There was the honeymooning couple, the Freezes, who had been at the hotel for four days and came in early each night to disappear into their room and not reappear until almost noon. They were not, Jasper assumed, watching a lot of TV. And there were the Philpots from new Jersey, who believed no one on the staff knew they were sneaking their Silky Terrier in through the north door. And, Jasper knew, no one at the hotel would confront them about it—unless the dog peed on the bedspread.

Jasper's curiosity about Mr. Jones had ebbed after the better part of an hour had passed and no unaccounted-for stranger had appeared. Idly he wondered if the woman had let her lover in through one of the side doors, like a pet. So when the house phone rang, Ms. Smith and Mr. Jones were not at the forefront of his thoughts.

"Front desk."

The distinctive, attractive voice greeted him. "Is this the concierge?"

He smiled. "Ms. Smith. Yes, this is Jasper. How may I be of service?"

"Jasper, do you know if you have a corkscrew available?"

"Oh, yes, ma'am." He pulled open the long, flat drawer beneath the counter and picked up the cheap, orange corkscrew he saw every time he opened the drawer. "We have one right here."

"Well, you're a college man," she said playfully. "Do you think you could figure out how to work it?"

"I believe so. Yes, ma'am."

"Okay. Well, come on up. Remember the number?"

"Yes, ma'am: 204. I'll be right there." He put the phone back in the cradle and picked up the walkie-talkie. "Manuel? Do you read this?"

Ten seconds later the handyman replied. "Hey, Jaz. What you need, *Jefe?*"

"Can you come down and watch the desk for a few minutes. I've got to run an errand for a guest."

"Right there."

True to his word, Manuel appeared within two minutes. He was wearing jeans and a black t-shirt and carrying a bag of cheese puffs. He plopped into Sol's office chair behind the desk and turned on the little TV.

"Enjoy, Jaz."

"I shouldn't be gone more than five or ten minutes."

"Whatever. Take all the time you need."

He climbed the stairs. Jasper had learned to avoid the slothful elevator, that—as Flo had warned—had a tendency to stop between floors once or twice a day and buzz loudly until someone tripped the breaker to restart it. The stairs, he thought, with their broad strips of frayed carpet, were actually more dangerous than the elevator.

Jasper wondered if this would be his chance to get a look at Mr. Jones. Maybe the lover was someone famous and would duck into the bathroom when the concierge came into the room.

He straightened himself as he stood before 204, took a breath and tapped lightly on the door. It opened instantly and the woman stood before him. She smiled.

"Did you bring that corkscrew?"

"Yes, ma'am." He displayed it dutifully with his right hand, his left hand behind him.

She stepped out of the way and he entered the room. As he passed beside her, it seemed to him she was not quite as tall as he had thought. Glancing down, he saw she had kicked off her heels. And he was surprised as well that there was no sign of Mr. Jones, who apparently had not yet arrived. The third surprise was that the room was dimly lit. Only the entry light was on.

"Over by the bed, on the nightstand," she said. "It's that $50 bottle of chardonnay."

Moisture had accumulated on the wine bottle. She must've brought it chilled in her valise, Jasper thought. He pulled the green foil from the top, revealing the cork, and pressed the point of the screw into the soft wood.

She sat down on the bed, her bare, crossed legs right beside where he stood. "Now my husband," she said matter-of-factly, "would say there is no bottle of chardonnay worth $50." She shrugged. "He says no real wine has to be chilled to be appreciated. But then, he's such a snob for cabernet sauvignon. There is plenty of pretentious, overpriced cabernet out there." Her foot wiggled and she glanced up at him. "What do you think, Jasper?"

He eased the cork out slowly, making certain not to spill a drop of wine. "Well, ma'am, I think it's difficult for us to estimate the worth of things we can't appreciate." The bottle emitted a soft popping sound as the cork slid free. "For instance, why would a blind person want to spend millions of dollars on a painting by Van Gogh?"

She giggled. "Well said. Arthur collects old sports cars. Sometimes he spends six figures for rusty old cars that won't even start. I confess, that passion is lost on me."

He gave a slight nod. "And compared to that, a fine carafe of chardonnay is a bargain at $50." He cradled the bottle in both hands and motioned toward the empty glasses on the nightstand. "May I?"

"Please do."

She watched him silently as he filled one of the glasses that, he realized, she also must have carried in her valise. He set the bottle on the nightstand and used both hands to present the glass to her.

Her eyes closed, she sipped the slightly amber, thick liquid. "Ah," she said softly. "Tiller Golden never disappoints." She took a long drink. "I can spring fifty for the wine and fifty for the room, but Todd couldn't shell out five for a corkscrew." She looked up at the concierge. "Do you understand why I called you up here to open the wine, Jasper?"

"Not really, Ms. Smith. I hadn't given it any thought."

She smiled at him, a lovely genial smile. "What a wonderfully concierge sort of answer, Jasper. You are so good."

"Thank you, ma'am. I'm glad to serve."

"Um hmm." Her eyebrows arched momentarily. "Well I had to ask for your help because I've been stood up."

"Oh. I'm sorry to hear that, ma'am. I would assume Mr. Jones has been called away on very important business."

She finished the wine quickly and put the glass on nightstand. "Fill it again, will you, dear?" She dropped back, lying on the bed, her arms splayed, her legs apart. "Actually, I think this is the end of the affair."

"Oh." He considered carefully whether or not he should respond to her words as he refilled her glass.

She propped herself on her elbows and watched him. Jasper watched her back from the corner of his eye as he poured the wine. How old was she? Her bearing was playful and girlish and not at all that of a woman in her mid-40s. Or older.

She took the second glass from him and studied it without lifting it to her lips. "This is something important for you to learn, Jasper. Partly because you're a concierge. I can assume I won't be the last woman you'll encounter whose lover has stood her up. But also because you're an attractive young man. Who knows what relationships you'll experience yourself?"

She sipped from the glass, then continued. "Love affairs have a shelf life, you know. In the beginning, they are so exciting. Your love is all you can think about. You can't wait for the next time you get to see him." She sighed. "then comes a time when you're making love and catch yourself thinking about some project you're working on at the office or the party you're going to attend the next weekend. When that happens, the affair is on the downward slide."

"Yes, ma'am."

Her shoulders arched upward in a brief shrug. "It can go on after that for months. Even years. But gradually the time between your encounters becomes longer and longer. . . . And neither of you complains that you scarcely get together any more. Finally there is something that disrupts one of your rendezvous. And you never reschedule it. . . . The affair is over." She glanced up at him. "That's what happened tonight. Can you believe that asshole Todd texted me? How tasteless to end a year-long affair with a text message."

Jasper looked down. "I'm sorry you're having to go through this unpleasant experience, Ms. Smith."

"Lorraine," she corrected him. Please call me Lorraine, Jasper."

16

"Yes, ma'am. Lorraine."

". . . I didn't text him back though. Instead I called him. I told him only a scared little boy would end a relationship with a text message."

"Good for you, ma'am."

"Then he said, 'Oh, I didn't mean for our affair to be over.' And I said, 'Well it is.' Then I hung up."

Jasper laughed, and immediately wondered if he should have. Wasn't it presumptuous and familiar on his part to laugh at her story? When they exchanged looks and she smiled easily at him, he sighed with relief.

"So, Jasper. I assume you didn't just go off and leave the front desk unattended."

"Oh, no. I paged my co-worker, Manuel." He lifted the walkie-talkie part way from his shirt pocket to display it for her. "He can preside over the extreme nothing that is happening on a slow Wednesday night until I get back."

"Manuel. Is he the Latin young man I've seen working around here?"

"Oh yes." Jasper nodded. "He came to New Orleans as a very young teenager with a group of Salvadorans a year or two after Hurricane Katrina. They were helping to rebuild the city."

"And he stayed?"

"Yes, actually he did. There are two different stories about that."

"Oh?"

He nodded. "There's Manuel's version. He says his group just up and moved to greener pastures and left him here."

". . . And?"

"And there's the version told by Flo, our housekeeper and Cajun superwoman."

Lorraine laughed. She drank from her glass.

"Flo says," he said slowly, "when Manuel's group got ready to move on to Texas for a job there, Manuel didn't want to go. So he ran away and hid out in the hotel. That's where Sol find him, hiding in the laundry room."

"How funny."

"And Sol made him work to pay for staying here. That was when he found out how mechanically inclined Manuel is. He can fix anything. Which is why all this ancient equipment works perfectly."

"I see. And this Cajun superwoman?"

"Flo."

"I'm guessing she's the little spitfire I see around here occasionally."

"Yes, ma'am."

Her eyebrows raised, she said, "She's very attractive."

"She is. Yes."

"Anything between you two?" She finished the wine and presented the glass for a refill.

"Hardly." He poured the wine into the glass she held toward him. "She has a young man named Anton she's in love with. She's told me that, should I look twice in her direction, my bloated body will be found floating in the canal." He made eye contact with the woman. "If you don't mind my noticing, Lorraine, you seem to know the hotel and its staff very well."

The girlish smile reappeared. "I have all my affairs here."

"Well. Very good. We certainly appreciate your business."

"I mean here in this very room. You want to know why?"

"Of course."

Her glass in hand, she hopped off the bed and headed for the window. She motioned toward the door. "Turn off that light, love."

Jasper set down the bottle, stepped toward the door, put his hand on the light switch and hesitated, looking toward the woman who stood at the window.

"Go ahead," she implored.

He cut off the light and the room instantly became completely dark. He heard the sound of the curtain sliding open and suddenly the image of the French Quarter at night became a glimmering, living mural before him.

He saw the motion of her silhouette move to the center of the wall-to-wall window. She twisted, looking over her shoulder at him. "Come here, darling."

Jasper moved slowly across the room, wondering if there were unseen obstacles on the floor. As he drew to within three or four feet of the window, he felt her grasp his hand and she pulled him to her side. As they stood, gazing out the window at the scene below, she made no effort to release his hand. Jasper decided a proper concierge would not reject the woman's grasp. He stood silently—

18

as calmly as possible—next to her, their hands joined.

"This is my second favorite view of Nola," she said quietly. "Standing here, you can see lovers, drunks, vacationers. Working girls. Con artists. Buskers. Street cleaners. . . . The whole experience of Nola lives itself out right before you."

She took a sip of wine and tightened her grip on his hand. "Do you know when I first saw this?"

"No, ma'am."

"When I was fourteen."

His eyes were acclimating to the dark interior of the room and he saw her broad, excited smile as she turned to him.

"You came here when you were fourteen?"

She nodded and gazed down at the street. My dad was in the hotel supply business. He brought my mom, my sister and me here while he met with Mr. Fontenay, who built and ran the *Plaisir* back in the day."

"How cool."

"My parents got their own room and they got this room for my sister Lou and me." She smiled. "Dad said it was so he wouldn't wake us with all his early and late phone calls. But I'm pretty sure it was so he and Mom could fuck without worrying about whether or not we could hear them."

". . . I see."

"Well it didn't take Lou and me long that first night to figure out what a killer view we had." She turned to him again. "Then I said, 'Lou, people on the street can't see us if we turn the lights off.' 'Yes they can,' she said, 'don't be stupid.' I said, 'I'll prove it.'

"So I told her I was going down to the sidewalk in front of the hotel. I said I'd wave at her when I saw her at the window. Then she was supposed to turn off the light and I could tell her whether or not people could see into the room from the street. She didn't want me to do it at first. I think mostly because I was in my pajamas."

He couldn't keep the surprise out of his voice. "You went down on the street in your pajamas?"

She nodded slowly. "Powder blue baby dolls. Barefoot. . . . That in itself was a lesson to me about New Orleans. Petty much nobody paid attention to me. Like a fourteen-year-old girl in baby dolls standing in front of a French Quarter hotel was the most natural thing in the world."

"I see."

"Well nobody else did. I mean, I saw Lou standing at this window and waved to her. The instant she turned off the light, you couldn't see anything inside this room. I couldn't wait to get back up here. I made her keep the light off. When people passed by on the street, we would pound on the glass. Sometimes they would look up, but they could never see us."

Jasper laughed. Lorraine renewed her grasp on his hand.

"Then I got an idea. I said, 'Lou, let's take off our clothes and stand at the window naked.'"

"Oh. And did you?"

She smiled. "Well, first it was just me. I was always the adventurous one. But when I stood there, totally nude, little sister decided to try it as well. . . . So we stood right here for twenty minutes or so, bare-beam and buck naked, pounding on the window as people passed by and totally invisible to the world."

Quietly Jasper said, "Sounds like you had fun."

"Oh . . . it got better. Lou was tired, you know. So she crawled up in the bed and went to sleep. . . . Not me. I was too excited. . . . So I stood here naked at the window. And masturbated."

Jasper once again was at a loss. He stood trying to decide what, if any, response he should make when she spoke again.

"Jaz, do you remember the last thing you said downstairs. 'If there was anything you could do to . . .'"

"Anything I can do to make your stay more enjoyable?"

"That's right," she said. "Did you mean that?"

"Of course, ma'am."

She dropped his hand and turned her back to him. "Then help me with this zipper, will you?"

He found the little fastener at the top of her dress and released it, then slowly lowered the zipper down the middle of her back. She bent her shoulders forward in response to his motion and the dress slipped silently to the floor. The woman stood, her back to him, clad only in a bra and panties that were very dark, probably black.

"Just lay my dress across the arm chair, if you will," she said. "It knows the scent of my clothes quite well."

Jasper spread the dress smoothly over the stuffed chair and turned back to the woman, who had not moved.

"You can work a bra clasp, can't you?"

20

"Yes, ma'am."

He unfastened the bra and slid it from her shoulders. She rubbed her arms across her chest, not so much to hide her breasts—since her back was to him anyway—as to move them and allow them to celebrate their release. He placed the bra atop the dress.

She looked back over her shoulder at him. "I don't have to explain what's next, do I?"

"No, ma'am," he said softly.

Jasper dropped to a knee behind her and took the lace top of her panties in the fingers of either hand. It was impossible for him to slide her panties over her hips and down her legs without touching her skin. One hand on the window, she pressed her thighs together. Jasper dropped the panties onto the chair.

"Ooo. This is so good. Just like all those years ago. I've been coming back for thirty-five years and doing this. . . . It never gets old."

She turned to face him. Without moving his eyes, he took in her breasts—long ovals and perfectly proportioned with the dark nipples sitting just a bit below the center of each. And below that he could make out the triangle of trimmed pubic hair.

Reaching out to him as she spoke, she began to loosen his tie. "Now what makes this better is to have a man's bare chest pressed against my back as I stand at the window."

Swiftly—amazingly so—she had his tie off and his shirt undone and then off him entirely and thrown aside. Grasping his hand with hers, she turned back to face the window, pulling his chest against her back. Slowly she wrapped his arms across her chest, his hands atop her hands directly above her breasts. Even without touching them, Jasper could tell how firm they were. She leaned back against him, raising her head and closing her eyes.

"You see," she murmured, "so much better than when I was fourteen."

He whispered in her ear. "Yes, ma'am. Only, I believe you said there was something more to it."

Eyes still closed, she smiled. She lifted his right hand to her lips and sucked in his index and middle fingers. At the same time, she put her hand on the back of his left hand and positioned it on her breast, his fingertips caressing the stalky nipple. Slowly, inexorably, she guided his right hand down from her mouth, the length of her

21

extended neck, between her breasts, along the gradual slope of her belly, across her abdomen to the intensely curly strands of hair on the mound of her pubis. There she stopped.

Jasper became aware of a tart, pungent aroma. It was, he recognized, the scent of the woman's arousal. He was, himself, burdened with an erection that had grown massive as he had watched and felt her prepare herself for this moment. He knew she could feel his heavy breathing on her neck. And, to be sure, she must have felt the arc of his engorged penis within his trousers.

She lifted her hand from his and used her wrist to press down on his right wrist. Lorraine wanted him to proceed on his own.

Deliberately, gently, he guided his two fingers through the patch of hair to the protrusion of her clitoris. She sighed and a shiver pulsed through her. Jasper pressed the tip of his index finger against her clit and ran his middle finger slowly inside her vagina.

It was slick—surprisingly wet. In his few experiences of touching vaginas, they had mostly been moist and only grew wet after stimulation. This was different. Lorraine's arousal was beyond his experience, and maddeningly arousing to him. He could feel the wetness spreading from his own member as he pressed against her.

He moved his middle finger back and forth deliberately within her. Her behind rocked in response. She placed both hands against the window to steady herself and spread her legs broadly to receive his touch. The silence in the room was broken by her quiet whimpering and his deep breathing. A tremor spread through her and she reached down with one hand and stopped the motion of his hand, holding his fingers deeply inside her.

"Oh. Oh. . . . Oh."

She leaned her head against the glass, her limbs limp and heavy. They stood together—his fingers within her vagina, his other hand on her taut nipple, her head down and her weight against the window—for a full minute. At length she took her hand off the glass and reached behind herself without looking. Deftly, with no wasted motion or fumbling, she unstrapped his belt, undid his pants and slid her hand inside his underwear from the top. She grasped his phallus, rigid and throbbing, with her wise fingers.

"Jaz, my darling?"

"Yes?"

"You . . . aren't allergic to latex, are you, darling?"

He shook his head. "Not at all."

Without letting go of his member, she turned toward him. She kissed him, open mouthed, slowly, filling his mouth with her tongue as she ran her fingers the length of his cock again and again.

"I think we've got to get you some relief." She kissed him again. "Otherwise . . . you might explode."

Quickly she went to the nightstand beside the bed. He heard the muted sound of her purse unlatch. In a moment she was back at his side. She deftly slid his pants completely down around his ankles, then knelt before him. He watched her manipulate a flat, square packet and heard it tear. She tossed the empty wrapper aside and held the condom to the glans of his member. There she hesitated for a moment, seeming to admire his penis.

"Oh my," she said girlishly. "Look at this brave, very tall soldier standing at attention." She rolled the condom over his erection. "We have to send this boy into action."

Lorraine turned away from him, assuming the same position before the window that she had held before. And, knowing what she wanted and expected—though feeling clumsy because of the pants around his ankles—Jasper came to her, putting his hands on her shoulders. It surprised him when he felt her hand reaching between her legs and grabbing his dick. She bent over a bit more and spread her legs farther, raising her behind. Jasper eased his hips forward and felt the sweet, electric delight of his member sliding fully into her passage.

Slowly he began to rock back and forth. This was, he confirmed silently, the most erotic sexual experience of his life and he wasn't sure how long he would last, especially with the woman moving to and fro in concert with him.

Then he became worried that he had injured her. She bent forward even more and placed her arms on the window sill and moaned loudly. In the next instant the walls of her vagina tightened on his penis, slowing his movements and surprising him.

"Oh. Oh . . . ," she whimpered, her tone almost pleading. Then she began to move her hips quicker and she began to speak to him in her delightful, girlish voice. "Jaz, my love."

"Yes, my Lo."

". . . I have a confession to make. . . . It's not anything bad, I think. It's that—"

She stopped almost completely, once again her inner walls tightening down on him. Jasper paused for a moment, then when he resumed his rocking motion he found his penis to be even harder and thicker.

"I was going to ask, have you ever heard of an easily orgasmic woman?"

His breath came urgently as he responded. "I don't think so."

"Well that's what I am. . . . I can pop and pop and pop again. I love to fuck."

Jasper thought he needed to respond, but wasn't sure what to say. "You . . . you have a magnificent body, Miss—uh—Lo. Making love to you is a beautiful experience."

She came again. Each time her limbs seemed to grow more flaccid. "Yes? What a nice thing to say. And may I say, you have an exquisite cock. And you know how to use it." She straightened slightly. "You haven't come yet, have you?"

"Uh, no ma'am."

She straightened a little, disengaging from him. "Well let's make use of this bed. It looks all lonely over here.

She took his hand and led him—shuffling, trying not to trip—to the edge of the bed, where she fell onto it backward, her legs splayed. It was difficult for him to decide what was the sexiest thing before him in that instant in the dim light: the roundish, crumpled flesh of her wet vagina, her nipples—erect despite her lying on her back—or the yearning, eager look on the face of this erotic woman desperate to be continually fucked.

Jasper had been close to coming, but the interlude of moving from the window to the bed allowed him to regain some composure. And when he entered her and she lowered her head against the sheets and arched her back, he had a feeling of sexual confidence unlike any he had ever experienced.

In a moment Lorraine had another orgasm. She looped her legs, lithe and toned, against his buttocks, holding him motionless within her. Then, surprisingly, she began to rock again, rapidly moving her hips, her inner lips tightening against him with a sort of desperate of clinging. She was, he realized about to have another, even fiercer climax. And this time he could not contain his own need to come. He heard himself moan and the sound of it aroused the woman even more. She squirmed beneath him, trembling and bouncing as in the same instant they came.

His motion continued for seconds afterward. He looked down at her, her eyes closed, a sublime expression of ecstasy on her face. He wanted to lie atop her, but thought better of it. Rolling to the side, he lay on his back, drawing great breaths, his eyes closed.

"Jaz."

He tried to calm his breathing before he answered. "Yes, ma'am."

"I'm so fucking glad Todd didn't show up."

He smiled. What would be a good, concierge response?

"Uh. I'm delighted to be of service, ma'am."

At length she rolled onto her stomach, studying his naked body with what seemed to him to be great appreciation. She put her hand on his chest and ran her fingers slowly down to his abdomen.

"So can I ask," she said, "where did you come from to come here for the apprentice program?"

"Idaho. Idaho Tech. I'm a rising senior. The apprentice program is one of my requirements to be certified as a concierge."

"You have a place in mind where you're going to be going."

He smiled and shook his head. "No. Not really. I had a girlfriend who was also in the program. Tracy was a year ahead of me. She ended up going to work for a motel chain out of Washington D.C."

"Does she want you to follow her?"

"No." He propped himself on his elbows, delighting in the unabashed nakedness of the woman beside him. "We were good for each other, but there wasn't a whole lot of magic there. We were colleagues-with-benefits, I guess you'd say. And when she graduated and I left for New Orleans, we understood it was all over."

Her eyebrows arched. "Well that surprises me."

". . . Why is that?"

"I'm just kind of surprised she would let a hunk of man like you get away."

He shrugged and said, "Sex wasn't a big thing with her."

"Obviously not."

He felt her fingertips caress his encapsulated penis. She was studying it as she rolled it back and forth on his belly.

"Just out of curiosity, how long does it take you to recover after you've had an orgasm?"

25

"Recover? You mean, how long before I can get another erection? Maybe five or six minutes."

She sat up on the bed. "Seriously?"

"Yes ma'am." He glanced at her and saw a sly smile creeping across her face.

"I'm going to have to feel that to believe it."

Chapter Three

Jasper heard the south hallway door open just after midnight, followed by the unintentionally silly sounds of a dozen young women trying to be quiet as they giggled and laughed aloud and bumped along the wall making their way to their rooms. He smiled and without looking up from the forms he was completing.

"Good evening, Tri-Beta," he muttered.

They had used their room key to come in through the side door, he knew, so he would not see the liquor bottles, party drugs and random pieces of contraband they were bringing with them to continue their sorority celebration. He wondered idly what sort of mess they would leave for Flo in the morning and whether they would make their 11 a.m. checkout time.

When the second of the adjoining room doors closed, their festive noises ceased completely. He assumed—and hoped— nothing would be heard from the girls until after his shift ended at 8 Saturday morning.

Jasper had not checked them in when they arrived earlier in the evening. It had been one of Tizzy's last chores and, histrionically she had described in lurid detail the appearance and the attitude of the girls in the group.

"I cannot get over how these girls dress these days," she had proclaimed, her eyes wide, her hands on her broad hips. "We had miniskirts in my day, but these girls—why those short, loose little dresses barely cover their asses. It's like they want the boys to see their underpants—if you can call those tiny things underpants." She shook her head in awed disgust. "There's no mystery and no real romance in that. Do girls dress that way in Idaho?"

"Of course not," he had replied. "You can't dig potatoes and bale hay in little black dresses."

"Oh!" Tizzy had pushed his shoulder. "You mock me, young man. You think I'm an old fogey."

"No, ma'am."

"Yes you do. You're just too polite to admit it."

"You're not a fogey and you're not old, Miss Tizzy. And if any of those girls come by the desk, I'll give you a full report on whether or not they are inappropriately dressed."

"You do that."

It had been a busy Friday evening and by 9 all the available rooms were spoken for. The lobby was quiet apart from people returning to their rooms from the French Quarter. Jasper sat on the tall stool behind the registration desk, his head tilted forward, apparently ignoring those who entered the room—though he was completely aware of everyone. The hard surfaces of the entry area meant that sound carried well, and he could overhear many whispered conversations—to none of which he reacted.

He heard muffled steps coming down the south hallway toward him about 12:45 and saw the young woman enter the lobby from the corner of his eye. Jasper realized immediately, because of her age and the short, emerald dress she wore, she was one of the Tri-Beta sorority sisters. He expected her to approach the desk and request a toothbrush or plastic cups or towels. Instead she slipped quietly into one of the thickly padded arm chairs that faced the registration desk and sat looking over her shoulder at the glass front doors.

Why was she just sitting there? He scooted papers around on the desk, not lifting his eyes while studying her closely.

She leaned back and raised her shapely legs onto the seat cushion of the chair, knees bent so her ankles were pressed against her behind. She crossed her arms over her chest. The girl was petite, perhaps 5'2" or 5'3". She had the proportions of a dancer or maybe a gymnast, with heavy, wavy, shoulder length wheat-colored hair. And the air conditioning in the lobby was clearly making her chilly.

Jasper pursed his lips. What would a proper concierge do in this situation?

He looked up at her and spoke. "Good evening, ma'am. How are you?"

"I'm fine."

He nodded. "Certainly. I do hope you will excuse me for bringing it up, but some guests find the lobby cool. May I give you a personal blanket?"

Her face brightened. "Oh yes, please. I'd like that."

He pulled one of the warming blankets from beneath the counter where Flo stacked them and walked around the desk as he unfolded it. Approaching her from the side, so that he would not be in a position to see her legs and short dress as she tucked the blanket around her, Jasper held open the blanket.

"Oh, thank you." She snatched it from him and instantly covered herself with it. "Oh, it smells good too."

"Yes," he replied as he went back to his stool. "Housekeeping prides itself on having everything perfectly clean and ready for our guests."

He took his place behind the desk again, then looked up as if noticing her for the first time. "I hope everything is all right with your room."

She leaned her head against the back of the chair. "The only think wrong with my room is that it's full of my sorority sisters."

"I see. Well. I'm not sure there's anything I can do about that."

A brilliant smile lit her face. For the first time he realized how intensely green her eyes were. Even in the lower lights, they picked up the fiery tint of her dress.

She shook her head. "I am so disgusted with them," she said slowly, smiling. She tilted her head to one side, studying him. "You don't look old enough to be running a hotel. You look like my age."

He nodded, looking down at his non-existent paper work. "I'm student, like you and your friends. I'm supposed to be in a concierge apprentice program this summer. That's why I'm here."

"You sure don't sound like you're from New Orleans."

He made eye contact, smiling. "I'm from Idaho. That's just north of Texarkana."

She laughed. Her voice was as cheerful as her smile. "We go to school up in Baton Rouge, Mr. Concierge. Idaho must be 2000 miles from Texarkana." She stared at his name tag. "Is your name really 'Jaz'?"

He smiled, gazing down rather than making eye contact. With her—so attractive and so close to his age—it was difficult for him to act the part of the concierge.

"My name is Jasper. The housekeeper decided that, since I'm in Nola, I should be called Jaz."

She gave him a faux squint. "I'm not sure that's dignified enough for you. It should be 'Mr. Jaz.'"

"Ha. I will pass that along." He sat up on the stool, watching her with his arms folded across his chest. "So, if you don't mind my asking, why did you leave the party?"

"Oh, disgusting." Her smile disappeared. "Could you hear us come in."

"Yes, of course."

"This just doesn't appeal to me." She took a deep breath. "Really it never did. My sister and my cousin were Tri-Betas ahead of me, so I was a legacy. I sort of had to go along with them. But I'm going to be a senior this fall and I just want to concentrate on graduating and getting ready for the real world." She glanced back toward the north hallway. "This is Tri-Beta's official you-made-it blast for last fall's pledges. And all they want to do is drink champagne and smoke mar—" She caught herself as she remembered to whom she was speaking, her eyes suddenly wide.

"Cigarettes," he said without changing expression. "We know people bring tobacco into the *Hotela Plaisir*. We don't say anything as long as it doesn't cause a problem with the other guests."

"Whew." She smiled. "I'm . . . really glad to hear that."

"Well," he shrugged, "the hotel must live up to its reputation." Jasper pursed his lips. "Champagne, you say?"

"Yes?"

"Usually champagne results in a lot of vomiting."

"Oh," she said, her face growing maternal, "you have our house card on file for those two rooms, Mr. Jaz. If the girls make any kind of a squatty mess, you charge us whatever it takes to clean it good as new."

"A 'squatty mess'? That's a new one." He chuckled. "I'm sure that won't be necessary." He worked to maintain eye contact, since the blanket had shifted and one leg, bare to her hip, presented itself clearly. "So, you're getting ready for a job search then. You mind me asking what your major is?"

"Secondary education. I hope to be certified in social studies, Spanish and French."

"Education is a noble calling, I would say. And if you can ride herd over your sorority sisters down the hall, I don't think high school holds much for you to fear."

She sighed and leaned back. She seemed weary. "I have two semesters of student teaching coming up. That will tell the tale. If I hate it—" she yawned, "—I'll go back to grad school and work on becoming a college professor."

"I apologize, ma'am," he said. "When I asked if your room was

30

acceptable, I should have asked your name."

She focused on him again with her sparkling eyes. "How clever of you, Mr. Jaz." She smiled. "It's Mattie. My name is Mattie Lewis."

He smiled back. "Yes. The name suits you."

"It's really Matilda," she said, smiling broadly. "I catch a lot of grief for that."

He shook his head. "No more than I get for being named Jasper."

They stared at each other. Mattie yawned.

"So, I'm going to teach," she said. "And you are going to run hotels?"

"I do hope to become a concierge at a fine establishment. Yes."

"That sounds so much sexier than teaching pimply teenagers."

He laughed. He started to tell her that she would make any classroom sexy, regardless of the subject, but caught himself.

"Mattie, you seem really tired. How about if I call down to your room and tell them there's been a noise complaint and say I'm coming down there in fifteen minutes? That will make them put away anything they don't want somebody to see and quiet down. Then maybe you can go back and get some sleep."

"No." She shook her head slowly. "If you call and then I go back down there, they're going to know I threw them under the bus. I have been too honest with them about my feelings, I'm afraid. They tolerate me because I'm on my way out." She tightened the blanket around her. "How about this. Let's use that sorority credit card to rent me my own room. I'm a Tri-Beta officer. I can do that, you know."

"Well that would be excellent, ma'am. Only we have no available rooms."

"Oh my god," she whined, closing her eyes and letting her head drop back against the chair. "Not even one broom closet."

Jasper studied her as she reclined against the chair. More than attraction for her, he felt sympathy.

"Actually there is a room."

She sat up straight, looking at him.

He reached under the counter for the third floor keys and produced the spare key to his room. He walked around to her chair and presented it to her. She gripped it and looked at the number.

"So here is the deal. Typically we don't let out the rooms on the third floor. Most are not up to code and we'd get shut down. Which is why I can't charge you for this room. However you will find it perfectly made up with clean sheets and towels and the other things you might need."

She rolled the key over in her hand and glanced up at him slyly. "And will I find your stuff in that room, Mr. Jaz?"

He shrugged. "Just ignore any personal items you might stumble across. I can assure you that the bedclothes are pristine and have not been slept in." He walked back behind the counter, trying to be as businesslike as he could and not think about the luscious young woman who was about to sleep between his sheets. "Would you like a wakeup call?"

She turned the key over in her hand coyly. "Where will you sleep?"

"Oh. Well, I get off at 8 in the morning. So you'll have at least seven hours uninterrupted. I can hang out down here if you want to sleep longer."

"No, no. You're being too kind already. I can be out of there by 8 and I won't need a call. I'll just get up and go back to our rooms. Those girls won't even hear me come in."

"Yes ma'am." He nodded toward her. "You can take the blanket with you, if you'd like."

She got out of the chair, the blanket around her shoulders and covering her to her waist. He marveled again at the exquisite shape of her bare legs.

"This is very gallant of you, Mr. Jaz," she said in a playful, marvelously sensual voice, "to let a total stranger have your room. To trust her with all your stuff."

"Well." He struggled to remain professional. "If you can't trust those who will be educating the leaders of tomorrow, who can you trust, Miss Mattie? If there is anything you need, if there is anything I can do to make your stay more pleasant, please don't hesitate to let me know."

Her voice was demur. "Thank you."

His head down, he watched from the corner of his eye as she went to the elevator door and disappeared.

The house phone rang at 7:50 a.m. He grimaced. Ten more

minutes and Sol would have been there for his Saturday morning shift.

"Front desk. May I help you?"

"Yes. This is room 312. Is it too early for room service?"

He recognized her voice immediately and smiled. "Miss Mattie Lewis. I trust you had a good night's sleep."

"I feel wonderful." She paused as she stretched. "So, seriously, no room service?"

"Uh." He chuckled. "Well, we don't have a restaurant. We do offer a complimentary continental breakfast in the seating area adjacent to the lobby."

"This isn't my first trip to the hotel of high pleasure, Mr. Jaz."

He remembered then that she spoke French.

"My sorority comes here every summer to get drunk and stoned."

"I see."

"As I recall, there is a little bagel and pastry shop just down the street a block or so."

"Yes. The *Petite Croissant et Café.*"

"Yes. That is the one. I would like an all grain bagel with veggie cream cheese and a small black coffee."

"I see. Well I'm sure, Miss Mattie, that would be available, however I'm not sure that little shop delivers."

"I bet you deliver."

He straightened, looking at the chair where Mattie sat the night before, wondering if she had really intended the innuendo or was just being playful.

Before he could speak, she said, "Here's my plan, Mr. Jaz. I believe you're going to get off in ten minutes. If you are willing—and I most certainly hope you are—I would like for you to take the number of the Tri-Beta credit card down to the bagel shop and get my breakfast. I'll wait here in your room for you to bring it up to me." Girlishly, she added, "Oh, and you can have whatever you'd like for yourself."

". . . I really don't see how a concierge can refuse a request like that."

She squealed. "Oh good!"

"So, if I come to the room by, say 8:15, will that be appropriate for you?"

33

"Mr. Jaz, can we just drop that whole 'appropriate' bullshit thing and be college kids?"

He laughed. "Yes, ma'am. At 8 a.m. I magically turn back into a guy."

"I'll see you then."

Five minutes later Sol appeared, unshaven and groggy. Jasper went over the non-events of the evening.

Flo, apron around her white stretch top and blue jeans, came to the desk. "So, either you want some breakfast?"

"Just coffee, girly," Sol said without looking at her.

"No, nothing for me," Jasper said. "I want to give you a heads up, Flo. I have it on good authority that the sorority girls down in 102-104 were drinking champagne last night. If they threw up all over the place, we can assess a cleanup fee."

She was holding the tongs she used to turn French toast and waffles and tapped her shoulder with the tangs, a curious expression on her face. "So how you know they drinking bubbly?"

Sol stopped as well, glancing at him.

"Oh," he said casually, "I could hear the corks popping."

Flo drew a skeptical breath. "Lot of popping goes on around here at night, Jaz man. Don't sound like corks."

"Well." Jasper straightened. "I am going to enjoy my day off. See you tomorrow night."

With that he headed out the big glass doors, down the street to the *Petite Croissant et Café*. The Hispanic woman behind the counter filled his order and keyed in the credit card number he had written down.

"So now you offer room service at the Hotel?" she asked.

"This is for a special guest," he said conspiratorially. "She wasn't able to stay in her room last night, so we're trying to keep on her good side."

"Oh. Okay."

Sol wasn't even behind the counter when he came back through the lobby. Jasper could hear him in the serving area, speaking to one of the guests.

Riding up in the elevator, Jasper was filled with electric anticipation and caution. What if the girl hadn't really been dropping sexual hints? What if she was someone who flirted, but had no intention of following through with her broad suggestions?

34

While that had been his experience through high school more than college, he had never known anyone like this incredibly alluring girl. He wasn't sure what she really wanted from him.

He knocked on his door, holding his breath in anticipation.

An instant later he heard her. "Don't you have a key, Mr. Jaz?"

He smiled. Cradling the drink tray and bag from the bakery, he unlocked the door and pushed it open.

The girl was still in his bed. That surprised him. He didn't know what to expect, but he hadn't expected that. Mattie was lying with her head on a pillow, facing the door, and when he came in and went to the little round table where he ate most of his meals, she sat up and stretched, the sheets up to her waist. She was wearing one of his white t-shirts and when she stretched the outline of her breasts and large nipples were easily visible. She ran her hands through her incredibly thick, full hair and shook her head.

Opening the sack and taking out their bagels, he said, "I hope you slept well."

"Oh my god, it was wonderful." She dropped back onto the pillow. "I didn't know you could sleep through the night at this hotel."

He opened the cream cheese. "Would you like me to serve you in bed?"

"Oh no."

She pushed back the covers and popped up. For an instant her green panties were plainly visible, then the long t-shirt dropped to cover them. She seemed totally at ease, knowing how much of her Jasper was seeing. Pulling out the extra chair, she sat across from him at the table.

"I remembered that bagel place from last year or the year before. I had to have their coffee to survive, but they put something in the bagels too." She took a bite and closed her eyes, cream cheese painting the outline of her lower lip.

Jasper fixed his bagel and leaned back in his chair. "Well we didn't hear anything from your sisters last night."

"You won't until about check out time."

"Do you think they'll make it up and out by then?"

"Oh, I'll make sure of that."

He took the receipt from the bottom of the bakery bag. "So I did what you told me and charged our breakfast to the sorority credit

35

card." He pushed the paper toward her.

"We are glad to pay for this," she said. "It's the least we could do, what with you giving up your bed."

"Well, I wasn't using it at all. I was glad . . . for you to have it." She looked around at the rumpled covers. "And what a wonderful bed it is." She looked back at him and tilted her head. "Is your girl coming from Idaho this summer? To share your wonderful bed?"

"Ha." He shook his head. "No. At the end of the last semester, she and I went our separate ways."

"Oh," she said. "How disappointing."

"It was mutual. No hard feelings." He looked up at her. "What about you? What does your guy think about you engaging in a night of all-girl debauchery in New Orleans?"

Mattie grinned, her marvelously expressive eyes squinting mischievously. "My guy is doing his summer abroad. In Australia."

"Wow. I guess you all . . . what, text? Skype?"

She shrugged. "No. Not much. They are not just on the bottom of the world but also on the other side of it. When it's day here, it's night there." She took another big bite, speaking as she chewed, "We tried communicating right at first, but it got to be too much of a hassle."

"I'm sure he misses you."

Her eyebrows arched. "I'm sure he does. He was dismayed to discover that his collegium group was 100% male."

"Sucks for him."

"He will be one horny little bastard when he gets back." She sipped from her coffee cup. "Of course, he's not back yet."

Jasper looked up at her to find her staring at him. She took another bite and dropped the remaining piece of the bagel onto the table. Leaning back in the chair, she stretched again, watching him as he glanced at her breasts.

"I found one of your t-shirts on top of your dresser there," she said. "I hope you don't mind. It was long enough to be a nighty."

"I'm glad it was helpful. I didn't even think about your needing a nightgown."

She shrugged. "Well, I would've gotten by without it, if need be."

Mattie looked back toward his unmade bed. She stood and

36

turned toward the bed and, wordlessly, pulled the t-shirt over her head. Then she bent over and pushed her panties down to her ankles, her perfectly proportioned round buttocks jiggling ever so slightly, and stepped out of the underpants that matched the emerald dress lying on the recliner. She went to the bed and scooted onto it, her back against the headboard and her legs casually apart. For a moment she stared at him.

Jasper swallowed. As he gazed unabashed at her round breasts, crowned with dark, half-dollar sized areolas and quarter-sized nipples, and let his eyes drop to the tufts of light brown hair shaved to a small triangle above the relaxed lips of her vagina, he concluded that she definitely had intended the sexual innuendo, that she definitely was not a tease.

"Want to come here?" she asked softly.

"I would love that," he replied, his face relaxing into a smile.

She held out her hand to him. He rose from the table and walked to the side of the bed, yanking off his tie and pulling his shirt from trousers.

"Here, let me help you with that," she whispered.

She leaned over and grasped his belt, undoing the latch and then the clasp of his pants and, without hesitation or haste, sliding down his zipper. Mattie scooted to the edge of the bed near him and put one hand inside his underwear to grasp his cock, as with the other she pulled his pants down to his knees. Watching her and having her undress him and touch him had caused him already to get a partial erection. She flopped his penis into the open where she could see it and wave it.

"Oh my," she whispered, "what a good boy you are."

And without another word she slid her mouth over his dick, her eyes closed, and sucked it, her tongue rough against the underside of it. It was so sudden and so arousing that he was alarmed. He knew he would not last long without climaxing if she continued.

She opened her mouth and her eyes, setting his member free as she looked up at him coyly. She milked a great, glistening drop of precum from the end of his glans and licked it off before it fell onto the sheets. Then she smiled at him.

"I have a question for you." Her voice was almost as arousing as her touch.

"Hope I have the answer."

37

"Once you come, how long does it take you to get hard again?"
He shrugged. "Five minutes. With you, maybe two minutes."
They laughed.

"Well, okay, if that's all it takes," she said, "I'll hold you to it
and we can proceed."

"Proceed?"

Mattie put his mouth back over his penis. She moved her head
back and forth with maddening slowness. His dick was slick with
her saliva and his own secretion. The motion and sensation seemed
to sap his strength. His eyes closed, he felt her put a hand on his
behind and encourage him to move his hips forward and backward.
She wanted him to fuck her mouth. It was excruciating and
magnificent and within a minute he came, an orgasm as hot and
explosive as any he had ever experienced.

He looked down to her in the instant afterwards. Clearly she had
swallowed the cum and had his member in her hand, pulling on it,
urging all the semen from it, which she took into her mouth with no
hesitation. Then she pulled him onto the bed beside her and, as he
lay recovering from the climax, she pulled off the rest of his clothes
so that he lay naked beside her.

"Are you okay?" she asked, inching her inches across his chest,
playing with his nipples.

"Uh, more than okay."

"That was certainly a great big wad you shot out of your big ol'
wiener, Mr. Jaz."

He drew a deep breath. "Was it?"

"Oh yes." She leaned against him, one warm, round orb resting
on his arm. "May I kiss you? On the lips?"

"Please do."

She leaned her weight on him has she pressed her lips against
his. In a moment her tongue slyly licked within his mouth. Jasper
could feel her hardness of her nipples against his chest and he
covered one breast with his hand.

"Ahh." She sighed and lay her head against his chest. "Thanks
for the kiss."

"The pleasure is mine."

"You know," she said slowly, "some guys won't let you kiss
them after they've creamed in your mouth."

He ran his other hand down the smooth slope of her back as he responded. "Sucks for them. I couldn't tell any difference. Of course, we hadn't kissed before that, but I'm assuming. . . . Actually I cannot imagine anyone turning down a kiss from you, whatever the reason."

She turned her head so she could see his face. "That wasn't your first blow job, was it, Mr. Jaz?"

He squinted. "Well . . . technically, I guess I could say no, that I've had oral sex before. But . . . let me say that this experience was so unique and unforgettable that I will henceforth measure any oral sex I have against what just happened."

Mattie giggled. "Oh, you're too kind."

He felt her hand on his member again, pulling it, elongating it. "That's not too sensitive is it?"

"No. Not at all. You can touch me all you want."

She got up on one elbow, childish eagerness on her face as she asked, "Do you want to play?"

"Sure."

"Okay. Sit up with your back to the headboard."

Jasper pushed and squirmed until he was pressed against the headboard of the bed. Mattie, her back to him, scooted backwards between his legs until he could feel his member between the cheeks of her behind. She took one of his hands and pressed it against her breast, the nipple instantly growing firm. She guided the other hand to her crotch and manipulated his middle finger against her clitoris. A shiver ran through her.

Her voice was barely above a whisper. "Got the idea?"

"Let's see," he whispered back.

Gently he moved his finger back and forth. Jasper felt her relax against him, her thick hair a pillow as she leaned back against his chest. He continued the motion for two or three minutes, then felt her hand on his again as she widened her legs and pressed his finger deeper within. She bent forward then, her hand still on his, pressing it upward and rocking her hips. He could feel his cock hardening again, twisted between them, but inexorably thickening.

"Oh, oh." She quivered. "Oh god, baby. Oh god."

Mattie stopped moving for an instant. "I think I feel wonder boy awake again," she said softly.

"Yes. He loves to play too."

She arced her back and leaned forward. He could see the

variegated pink and purple lips of her vagina as he settled her behind gently on his thighs and felt the gradual penetration of his cock. Again she begin to rock.

"Oh baby. . . . Yes. . . . Fuck baby."

As she raised and lowered herself onto him, even with the incredible arousal he was feeling, Jasper was confident he could keep going for a while without another climax. His first orgasm had prepared him for longer, wilder intercourse. And then the girl surprised him by stopping. She pulled herself onto the bed and turned to face him, her magnificent body naked and expectant.

"Mr. Jaz," she said her seductive, girlish voice, "I have a little confession to make."

"What's that?"

"You see, I have this oral thing. I just love oral. I especially love sixty-nine." She studied his face. "Are you good with that?"

"Well, let's just see how good I am with it."

She squealed. "Let's."

As he slid down the bed so his head was on the pillow, she turned to face the foot of the bed and crawled backwards over him. Her vagina, the lips ripe and moist, descended onto his face. He took her cheeks and spread them slightly and sucked her clitoris into his mouth. She quivered and moaned and in the next instant he felt her take his penis into her mouth and begin to move her head back and forth.

He slid his tongue repeatedly over the protruding clit, then slipped it as deep into her canal as he could. And there the liquid of her arousal poured onto his taste buds, rich and hot. With his middle finger he stimulated her clit again. She reacted so instantly that at first he thought she would pull away. Instead she moaned, her mouth still loose around his engorged cock. Her limbs seemed to weaken. Jasper felt the walls of her vagina tighten against his tongue as she quivered and came. She took his penis from her mouth, cradling it gently in her hand, and laid her chest on his legs. She was, he decided, recovering from an orgasm as mighty as the one she had given him.

"Okay," she said quietly. "Now it's my turn."

Mattie ran his member, lubricated with her saliva, between her breasts, then descended on it with her mouth. Her head ratcheted up and down as she sucked and salivated on him. The rapidness of his approaching climax startled him. He almost wanted to stop her, not wanting their sex to end. But the desire and the arousal was too great. He felt his back arch as he came in her mouth once more and then flatten onto his bed, breathing rapidly.

Mattie sat up, her behind on his stomach but her weight on her arms. She too was catching her breath.

"Well . . .," she said at length, "that was a fuck of a lot better than champagne and marijuana."

"I'll take your word for it," he muttered.

She turned and stretched out on top of him, their wet genitals sagging against each other. Her eyes, focused on his, were full of green mischief. She smiled.

"Thank you for letting me use yours."

"My . . .?"

"Why, your bed of course. This could never have happened in the room with the girls."

"I'm delighted to accommodate you. . . . And I can assure you, the pleasure was all mine."

"I think we did a good job of sharing," she said, in the tone a teacher would use with her classroom. "And none of those Tri-Beta bitches will feel near as good going home today as I will." She tilted her head to one side. "You know, as I've been whining all day and night about my sorority, you really haven't said anything. I'm guessing you're not a Greek?"

He shook his head slowly. "No. I hope you don't hold it against me, Mattie, but I just never could get excited about the fraternity thing. A couple of my buds back at Tech were in in Mu Ep, but it seemed to me like all they ever got for it was a constant hangover and they were always begging me for notes because they had missed class."

"Yeah, if you're not into drama, social climbing and begging your parents to give you money for pointless bullshit, I'm not sure Greek life is for you. . . . And I'm out of it after next spring."

Her studied her, awed by her flawless skin and proportions. "I envy your boyfriend. If I had been him, I would never have gone to Australia without you."

She shrugged. "What is that saying, 'familiarity breeds contempt'? I think he just got used to me."

Again he shook his head. "Oh my god. Is he defective?"

41

She giggled. "No. He's just . . . easily distracted. He'd kind of a careerist. You are too, you know. If you and I were a thing in Idaho and I asked you to stay with me rather than doing a concierge apprenticeship, would you have done it?"

Jasper leaned toward her. "If I had known it was going to be in this crummy, fleabag, roach trap, I would have."

Mattie looped her arms around his neck. "You say the nicest things." She held his eyes with her sparkling green eyes. "Got one more pop in you?"

He could not hold back the smile. "If I can put it in you."

Chapter Four

Jasper was standing behind the check-in counter with his back to the lobby when the bell dinged and the elevator door rolled open. Bent over at the waist, he was digging a roll of register tape out of the office supplies when he heard a woman's cheery voice.

"Well, what do you think?"

He straightened and turned toward the voice, where he saw an extremely pretty woman in her mid 30s standing before him with a great smile and her arms spread. The instant she saw him—and obviously recognized he wasn't the person she was expecting—the smile disappeared and her eyes grew round. She pulled her arms against her chest. Jasper took her in at a glance.

"Oh! Oh!" she exclaimed, then softly, "I'm so sorry."

"Good evening ma'am," Jasper said. "If I don't miss my guess, you were expecting to see our manager, Sol. Unfortunately his shift ended at 8 this evening."

Clearly she didn't know how to respond. She stared at him uncertainly.

"While I am not the man-of-the-world that Sol is," he continued casually, "I do have some observations I would be glad to share."

". . . You do? Well, sure. Please."

He nodded. "To begin with, your lovely turquoise blouse is a color well-suited for you, ma'am. It picks up the gray-blue of your eyes. Your flats match the blouse perfectly—which is especially difficult with shades of blue—and speaks to a certain understated elegance. The white slacks accent your very attractive form just as you'd wish and are the right seasonal length and weight. The silver clutch is the right size and color. Your makeup is scarcely apparent, demonstrating real attention with no overstatement. And . . . finally, I would note that the way you've done your hair, with the multiple parts, while it is relaxed and attractive, also reveals that you are a natural blonde."

Her jaw had dropped open as he spoke and, when he finished, her broad smile returned. "Thank you. Thank you so very, very much."

"It was all quite obvious, ma'am. I'm only sorry Sol isn't here. He would have added things I missed, I'm sure."

She closed one eye, skeptically. "I seriously doubt that."

"And let me say, ma'am, whoever you'll be meeting tonight will be absolutely delighted."

"I don't know about that, either," she said. "I guess it depends on who he is." She squinted at him. "This is probably way out of line, but . . . can I ask you a personal question?"

"Of course."

"Are you gay?"

Jasper tried not to laugh. "No ma'am. I'm a concierge. We're allowed to notice those sorts of things without being gay."

"Oh. Okay then."

"I hope you have a most pleasant evening, ma'am."

"Thank you."

He was filled suddenly with a protective yearning toward her. "Please consider us a resource for yourself throughout your stay in New Orleans, ma'am. If you need local information or if I can do anything to make your visit any more pleasant, please do not hesitate to let me know."

Jasper felt as if his words were empowering her. She seemed to have acquired a degree of confidence she did not have before. Or perhaps she was just trying to appear confident. For him, or for herself?

He watched her as she walked out the big glass doors. She paused once she stepped onto the sidewalk in the gathering dusk. She was, he recognized, trying to decide which way to go.

"Who are you and what are you up to?" he asked softly.

As she disappeared in the general direction of Bourbon Street, Jasper began to piece together what he could discover about the woman. Clearly she had checked in alone that day. She was intent on going out to enjoy the French Quarter night life with no apparent intentions, preferences or even awareness of precisely what she was seeking.

"What woman comes to Nola by herself on a Wednesday night, wants to go out and party without having anyone to go with or anyplace in mind to go?"

He began to search through the registration cards for her information. It was only a moment before he singled out the registration that had to be hers: "Miss Elizabeth Durbin, Longview, Texas; one evening prepaid."

Jasper straightened, still filled with curiosity. There were women, as he had discovered, who came to New Orleans alone or in small groups seeking adventure in a multitude of ways. He had witnessed that they seemed to know exactly what they were after. Each had a sort of determination and focus. Moreover, as he had seen, they almost all seemed to find who or what they were seeking. This woman, though, was different. She had a quality about her of . . . innocence. She seemed innocent to him, an ingénue?

When he looked down at her name on the registration card, it came to him that she had signed her name "Miss." "Miss Elizabeth Durbin." When was the last time, he asked himself, that any woman had signed the register as "Miss"?

Scarcely past 10 p.m. the glass doors burst open and lovely, nearly panicked Elizabeth Durbin dashed into the lobby. She glanced over her shoulder once as she ran toward the elevator.

Someone, Jasper realized, was following her. And as she reached out for the elevator call button, he spoke quietly, but distinctly.

"No ma'am!"

When she turned to him, he could see the fear. He nodded.

"Behind the elevator. Take the stairs. They're much quicker."

She turned and disappeared from his sight. He heard three or four steps on the staircase, then from the corner of his eye saw the glass front doors open again.

This time the person who came in was a man Jasper recognized, a fellow in his late 40s who typically stood somewhere on Bourbon Street or Market Street or any other touristy place around the quarter with a huge hurricane tumbler in his hands. His calling in life, as Jasper had observed, was harassing tourists. He would stand in front of one establishment or another, making vulgar comments and suggestive remarks until the proprietor of the store or the police approached him—at which point he would quickly turn and walk away. When Jasper saw him, he immediately understood the woman's distress.

"How are you, sir? Would you like room for the evening?"

"What? No. Where's the girl?"

"I beg your pardon?"

"I say, where's the girl."

"Oh, the young lady who came through the lobby a minute ago—blue top, white slacks?"

"Yeah, that's her. She's a honey, son."

Jasper nodded. "I thought myself she was very attractive. Were you supposed to meet her?"

"No, dude! I'm just trying to hook up. I'm pretty sure that's what she's after." He glanced around the big room. "I'm going to help her out."

"Well if you're intending to catch up with her, sir, she headed out the south lobby door." He pointed to the exit on the far side of the dining area.

"What's out there?"

"That's mostly a public parking lot. I guess her car is out there."

The man began to directly toward the door.

"If you catch up with her, sir," Jasper called after him, "we do have a room for two available."

The rascal had gone out the door already when he yelled back, "I got my own place, asshole."

Jasper shook his head and said beneath his breath, "Yes, but most outhouses only have room for one."

A full minute passed—Jasper standing behind the counter, watching for the man to come back—when he heard movement on the stairs behind the elevator, then rising footsteps. The woman had knelt on the stairs, he realized. She had listened as he misdirected the man who came looking for her. Her steps up the stairs were slow and measured, deliberate.

He had been right, Jasper decided. This woman was far too innocent to be alone in New Orleans.

As the evening passed, he began to believe the troublemaker was not going to come back into the hotel. He settled into his ritual of going onto the internet to check out the great hotels and resorts and letting the hours flow by, at least he was until just before 1 a.m. when the house phone rang.

"Front desk."

This time the woman's voice was far more sedate. "Is this the concierge?"

"Yes, Miss Durbin, this is Jasper. How may I help you?"

"Um. Would you be able to come up and speak to me sometime before you go off duty? Just for a minute? I wanted to say 'thank you' and explain what happened tonight."

"Certainly ma'am." He reached for the walkie-talkie. "If it's appropriate, I can come up in about five or ten minutes."

"I would really appreciate it. I'm in—"

"Room 210. Yes ma'am. I'll be there shortly."

It had been over a week since he had to call Manuel for any sort of help at night, something the handyman greatly appreciated. When Tizzy had the night duty, she constantly had him running errands, the sort of trivial things that Jasper did for himself.

"Do you copy, Manuel?"

Ten seconds passed, then, "Hey, Jaz man."

"Can you sit at the desk for me for a few minutes?"

"All depends, man. Just how good looking is she? Why don't you ever send me to take care of the lookers, man?"

"Well, she didn't want me to mention this, but it's your mother, Manuel."

"Aye, aye, aye! Don't even say it. I'm on my way."

As he waited, Jasper began to go over in his mind how he could console the woman without making her feel foolish. What he still did not understand was why a person so inexperienced as she obviously was would venture alone into the night life of Nola. All possibilities considered, what happened to her at the hands of the irritating fool was nothing compared to what might have happened.

"Here I am, lover boy."

"Thanks, *senor*. I'll be right back."

"Whatever."

He went up the stairs and down the hall to room 210. He stopped before the door and tapped lightly. It was only a few seconds before it opened.

She was wrapped in a large, pure white bathrobe, all makeup gone from her face and her hair wet and straight from a recent shower. As she backed away from the door and held it open for him, he could tell she had been crying. And once more he was seized by the desire to protect her.

"Please," she said, motioning toward the round table, "come in and sit down."

"Certainly, ma'am."

She pressed the robe tightly against her as she sat on the side of the bed. "Did you say your name is Jasper?"

"Yes, ma'am."

"But you go by 'Jaz'?"

He smiled. "My co-workers believe that 'Jaz' sounds a lot more New Orleans than 'Jasper' does, Miss Durbin."

She nodded and sucked her lips into her mouth momentarily. She had the look of someone who had been preparing an explanation.

"My name is Beth. Durbin. Yes. Beth Durbin. It's not Beth Robbins anymore. It's Durbin again."

Jasper sensed that the most important thing for him to do was just listen. Maybe to ask the occasional question for clarity, but basically just listen.

"You can probably tell, this is my first time to New Orleans."

"Yes, ma'am."

"I came down here to celebrate." Her tone was the sort one might use in explaining to a police officer exactly why one was speeding. "I'm here to celebrate my divorce."

"I see. Well, congratulations, ma'am, if that's in order."

She stared at him for a moment, then anxiously hopped off the bed and began to pace through the room. Filled with curiosity, he followed her with his eyes.

"Let me back up, if that's okay." she said, staring at the invisible path on the floor she was following. "My husband—my ex-husband—Ronny and I got married when we were only a year out of high school. Originally, we're from Beaumont, Texas." She glanced at him to make certain he was paying attention to her words. "He was my first real boyfriend. We dated from the time we were juniors until after we graduated. We actually got married in the summer before he started school in Commerce. We lived off campus and I worked while he got his degree. Then he got a job in Longview. I guess I was twenty-three and then twenty-five when we had our two girls. Steph and Sally are nine and seven now."

"Yes, ma'am."

"So after Sally was born, Ronny encouraged me to go to college myself. . . . Which I did. And I got my bachelor's in design. And I actually got a job."

She glanced up at him and he nodded.

"Then I thought, well, with both us working and two beautiful girls, it was going to be 'happily ever after.' . . . Until about six months ago when Ronny came home, sent the girls to spend the night with some of their friends, and told me he wanted a divorce. . . ." She sat down on the foot of the bed, her long, smooth legs at last motionless and clearly visible.

At length, he responded. "I'm sorry, ma'am. That must've been a terrible shock."

She raised her shoulders. "Oh, the shocks were just beginning. I pretty much perfectly followed the script of every naïve young wife. . . . I pleaded with him not to leave. I told him I wanted a chance to work on our problems, whatever they were. And I begged him to go to counseling, which finally we did."

". . . I take it that was not helpful?"

"Ha." She seemed to grow stronger, caught up in the story and intent on pouring forth the details. "We got nowhere in counseling. Every week we had the same discussion and when we went home, Ronny just avoided me. He was never willing to work on any of the communication techniques the therapist suggested. . . . Then one day at work—and I have to say, I hadn't told anybody, not one of my co-workers, what was happening between Ronny and me—one day one of the girls I work with came to me and said, 'You know, when somebody doesn't invest themselves in counseling, I've heard it's usually because there's someone else involved.'" She shrugged. "Well, I was stunned that she not only knew we were having trouble, not only knew we were in counseling, but also knew it wasn't working." She faced Jasper. "But I pushed all that aside right then and asked her, 'What do you mean?'

"She says to me, 'I mean Ronny is sleeping with the cute little Spanish girl in his accounting department.' . . . And I said to her, 'How can you know that and I don't know that?' And she said, 'Maybe you didn't want to see what was happening.'" Her head dropped. Slowly, wearing an expression of resignation, she nodded. "Then things began to add up. I realized that he was having sex with Luisa. And pretty soon I realized she was the just the latest. I began to recognize the signs I had been missing—or ignoring—and I realized Ronny had been having sex with different girls for years, maybe even before he graduated from college. In fact, the younger they were, the more he liked them. . . . I guess I was too old for him.

I was damaged goods, I guess."

Jasper started to correct her, but decided to wait and let her continue.

"In fact, I realized he had been with so many that I wondered if Starlene—the girl who told me what was going on, or I should say, made me face what I had been blind to—I wondered if Starlene had been involved with him too. So I went to her and asked if she had slept with him. And Starlene said, 'No. I never get involved with players, Beth. I could see Ronny coming a mile away and knew he was trouble.'" She nodded again. "I guess that's when I knew just how much of a scoundrel my dreamboat really was. And that's when I knew just what a sucker I had been."

When she looked at him, Jasper said quietly, "Yes, ma'am."

"This next part may ruin your opinion of me, I don't know." She shifted on the bed, unconsciously uncrossing and re-crossing her luscious legs and uncovering a bit more of them. "You see, I figured out what Ronny was and what he had been doing, but as far as he knew I was still this foolish hair brain who wanted to work things out. All the while he was sneaking Luisa off at lunch every day and screwing her brains out. Well, I had my own secret liaison—with a divorce attorney. There may not be any alimony in Texas, but that doesn't mean there aren't ruthless lawyers who know how to help their clients get what they need."

She paused, head down, reflecting. "So I changed around our finances to the extent I could without him knowing about it and I made some decisions about what I wanted when we went our separate ways. . . . Then, just about the time school was out for the summer, I sent my daughters to stay with my mom and I made a really nice supper. He was surprised about the meal. It was his favorite. Beef tips. And about the time he got through eating, he looked around and said, 'Where are the girls?' And I gave him a big smile and told him that I had filed for divorce. And I told him what I wanted and the child support he was going to pay and where he was going to move."

She fell backward on the bed. The robe rode up just a bit, enough for Jasper to tell she was wearing no underwear. For her part she seemed oblivious to anything but continuing the story.

"He was so stunned. . . . Literally he was speechless. And then the *coup de grace*. I told him that I had packed a bag for him and that he was leaving. Right then. 'Don't worry, Ronny,' I said. 'I'll take care of the dishes. Like always.' And he says, 'Well, where am I supposed to go?' And I said, 'I'd suggest Luisa's. She'll be glad to see you. Until she hits twenty and you start fooling around on her.'" She propped herself up on her elbows. "He couldn't get out of there quick enough. . . . And as I washed the dishes, I cried." She looked at Jasper. "That was the last time I cried over him."

He nodded. "Yes, ma'am."

She got up and stretched and began to a pace again. "After that, it went pretty much like the attorney said it would. She also told me I needed to spend one night a week with my girlfriends. That that would keep me from getting too depressed. . . . So I took her advice. Starlene and her friends weren't by nature the sort of girls I would have associated with, you know. But they have turned out to be just what I needed."

"I see," he said quietly.

She walked slowly toward the window as she spoke. "They're really what prompted me to come here tonight." For a moment she peeked out of the curtain onto the street below. "Every week we go to this little restaurant that's mostly a wine bar and they save us a table. We laugh and cut up. I have been able to relax with them and tell them things about myself that—" She shook her head. "—I would never have told anyone in a million years."

"Yes, ma'am."

She turned toward him, leaning against the curtain. She pulled the robe tightly about herself.

"Well what happened is this." She was looking past him, not making eye contact. "During one of our conversations in the café, it came to light that . . . Ronnie wasn't just my first. . . . He was my only." She looked up at him. "You know what I'm saying?"

He nodded, expressionless. "Your husband was the only man you'd ever made love to."

She nodded. "Yes. Well. When my friends got hold of that, they were amazed. I guess, though, I was too at what they told me next. I thought most people were . . . like me. But every one of those girls had multiple—some of them many—partners and they could not believe that I had only had sex with one guy in my whole life." She looked at him then. "I guess we had shared several bottles of wine at that point. They started telling me about their sex lives and who they had been with." She pursed her lips, glancing down. "It was really quite funny. A couple of them figured out that they had both had sex with the same guy and they were comparing notes, I guess you'd say. And then—" Her eyes grew wide. "—they started describing different guys and how they made love. I guess—" She shrugged. "—all guys are a lot different. You should have heard the things they were saying about what different guys did and wanted and would and wouldn't do. . . . That was a whole different kind of sex education for me."

When she raised her eyes to his, he nodded. "Yes, ma'am."

She pulled the robe against her again. "Then, and I didn't think it was possible, it got even more interesting. They started telling me that I needed to go out and experiment sexually. They said I was really short-changing myself by only sleeping with one guy. Then they started trying to figure out who they should fix me up with. They were actually debating whether or not they should encourage their boyfriends or even their husbands to have sex with me—like I say, they were pretty drunk. And it got even funnier. They would say, 'I'm sure so-and-so would take Beth to bed, but he's not that good and I really want her to get off.' And one of them said, 'I know who she'd like, but if she does him she'll steal him from you, Jessica.' And they giggled like crazy and Jessica says, 'Oh, take him, please. Screwing is all he's good for.'"

She sighed. "They were really after me to go out right then and find someone to sleep with. So I told them that I wasn't going to have sex with anybody until after the divorce was final. That way, I could always say I had been faithful. And also, Ronny wouldn't have anything he could use against me if it came down to it. . . . But the girls were relentless. They pestered me about when I was going to be with a man. And I said, 'As soon as the divorce is final. Right then I'm going to go someplace romantic and find the most handsome, sexiest man I can and take him to bed.'" She looked up at him. "So my divorce was declared legal this morning. I got everything I demanded. And I sent my girls to spend a couple days with my parents and came to New Orleans to get laid." She bit her lip. "Does this make me sound like a whore?"

Jasper could tell from her expression she was not joking. It took all his resolve to not laugh aloud or show any hint of a smile.

"May I respond frankly, ma'am?"

"Oh please do." Her expression was open, almost pleading.

"Very well. First of all, while you are a grown woman in your thirties and you have two children and have had some real-world painful experiences—" He shook his head slowly. "—I think you are about the most . . ." He searched for the word. "Undespoiled. I think that's it. I mean pure. Undefiled. You have great integrity regardless of any sexual activity you've ever had or ever thought about. Then there is the fact that you've only been with your husband. By definition, you cannot be a whore." He tilted his head slightly toward her. "You realize, of course, that people of loose morals don't even worry about something like that."

Her face softened, her mouth dropping open.

"And may I say, ma'am, that if you should follow through on the challenge you've placed before yourself here in Nola, that will not change you. You will still be the same, very worthy person you are and you should feel no regret whatever."

He squinted, considering his words, aware that she was paying attention to the nuance of everything he was saying.

"Also, I believe you expressed some concern that someone's opinion of you might be diminished because you secretly contacted an attorney and plotted against your philandering husband. May I say, ma'am, that I personally consider it an act of self-preservation and also of maternal care that you did what you did. . . . I think some people would not have been able to recognize the obvious hopelessness of the situation—that your husband was not going to change and that he was going to continue to play on your goodness as long as it suited him. You realized that—" He nodded. "—and you made decisions that were best for you and for your daughters. Yes, Miss Durbin, it's clear to me you have nothing at all to feel bad about. And I feel nothing toward you but admiration."

She stood at the window, arms across her chest, staring at him silently for so long he began to think he had said something terribly wrong. Then she sighed deeply and seemed to relax. And he did as well.

"That's the third time tonight you've rescued me, Jasper," she said.

"Rescued you?"

She lifted and lowered her head in a slow nod. "First with those incredible compliments about my outfit when you first saw me.

Then you saved me from that—guy who followed me."

He permitted himself a broad smile.

"And then just now, when you—so eloquently—approved of everything I've done."

He shook his head. "I'm not deserving of the right to approve or disapprove, ma'am. Everything I've said, however, is true and I hope you are able to . . . accept all the goodness in you, because it is so apparent to everyone else."

Something like a wave of relief spread over her and she leaned back against the curtained window. For the first time since he had come into the room she seemed almost comfortable.

"If you don't mind my asking, ma'am," Jasper said, "there is one thing I really don't understand."

"Oh?"

"Well, I know you went out looking for adventure, as they say, but you're an extremely classy woman. How in the world did you get involved with that reprobate who followed you into the lobby?"

"Oh!" She closed her eyes and smiled and spoke in staccato, "No, no, no, no, no! Allow me to explain what happened."

She crossed the room slowly to sit back on the foot of the bed near him.

"After we spoke downstairs," she said, "I went walking down the street three or four blocks and I came to hole-in-the-wall wine bar with a possum on the sign."

"*Vin Creole*."

"Yes. That was it. I thought that looked as likely as anyplace I had seen. So I took a deep breath and sat at the bar and ordered a glass of Chablis. And that kind of worked, I guess. Before too long I was talking to a couple—well, three—guys. We were laughing and they kept offering to buy me another glass of wine." She shrugged, her hands in the big pockets of the robe that had ridden to her creamy upper thighs. "I guess there was nothing wrong with those guys. They all seemed, you know, acceptable. I guess—" She wiggled her behind, staring beyond him as she recalled the scene. "—they thought I was acceptable too." She glanced at him. "My plan probably would have worked with any of those three fellows."

". . . But?"

"But somehow, none of them was just the right fellow." She took a deep breath. "This is going to sound crazy as hell, but as I've

54

been thinking about this, I'm sort of like a virgin again. In a way this is a new 'first time' for me. And none of those guys struck me as first time material, if you know what I mean."

"Yes, ma'am."

"So I finished my third or fourth glass of wine and I used the 'magic escape tool.'"

He grinned. "The 'magic escape tool.' I never heard of that one."

"It's a little lie women tell that always works. I said, 'I've got to go, boys. This is my time of the month.' And like magic they all backed off right away."

"Oh. I guess I have heard that one."

"But when I walked out the door, that strange street person was standing outside. He saw me and started talking to me right away, even though I never said a word to him. He is incredibly vulgar. He said, 'You're by yourself in the French Quarter? There's only one thing you can be here for.' And he kept following me and saying the ugliest things."

"Yes, ma'am," Jasper said. "That guy has been chased away from every establishment around here. He offends every visitor he gets within ear shot of, especially women. Although, I've never heard of him actually following anybody before. He must've found you most attractive."

"Well I sort of scurried away from him. He didn't want to run—mostly, I think, because he was afraid of spilling his drink. So I managed to get about 100 feet ahead of him by the time I got back to the hotel." She smiled. "Then you saved me from him."

He smiled. "It's all a part of the concierge service, ma'am."

"Jasper . . . you know . . ." She drew a quick deep breath through her teeth. "I didn't exactly tell you everything."

As he gazed at her it came to him that she wasn't going to say anything else until he responded.

"Okay."

". . . You know, I suppose, if someone is intent on just going out and getting laid, if you'll excuse my language, she probably shouldn't be all that picky. But I guess I am." She studied his face. "It's like I said. It's sort of the first time for me all over again."

"Yes, ma'am."

"So as I was standing there with those guys at the possum bar,

I realized that I wasn't just interested in a clean-looking man with an erection. . . . I was really looking for someone who was very good looking. Someone who was intelligent. Someone who was a gentleman and could carry on a conversation that was more than just suggestive innuendos and meaningless banter. And as I stood there listening to them, it occurred to me that I'd already met the right fellow." Her head drifted to the side so that she had an almost girlish look. "I left the bar to come back to the hotel to see you, Jasper."

He stared at her, unsure of how to respond. She stood and paced toward the window, then turned back toward him.

"But then that awful man started following me and I just ran into the hotel to escape from him. When you tricked him into leaving and saved me that way, I felt so foolish, like everything about my being here was just stupid. I felt so childish. I thought I could never approach you. . . . I spent the last hour up here going back and forth about telling you all this and . . . and asking you if you'd be willing to make love to me."

Jasper gazed at her, his mouth open, trying to find the right reply. She seemed to think his delay in responding was reluctance or unwillingness.

Looking down, she said, "I know I'm a lot older than you. And maybe—maybe you have a girlfriend or a fiancé or someone you're really committed to. But I'm not trying to come between you and anybody. This is just a one-time—"

"Beth." He cut her off. "May I call you 'Beth'."

"Of course."

"Beth, I don't have a girl. I want to tell you something I learned a long, long time ago—long before I became a concierge. I learned that, if someone offers you something precious, something beautiful that you know you don't deserve, you should accept it. Accept it right away. Say 'yes.' Take it before they change their minds."

She smiled slowly. "Oh."

"There is one other thing," he said. "While ago you said something about yourself. You said you were 'damaged goods'."

"I said Ronny thinks that."

"Well if he does, he's a damn fool and dead wrong." Jasper shook his head. "In case no one ever comes right out and tells you, Beth, you are the complete package. You're smart as hell. You're a professional. You're funny and gentle and loving and incredibly attractive. In fact—" He glanced at the robe, then back to her eyes. "—I was going to say you are perfect. But, frankly, I haven't seen enough of you to know that for sure."

Gradually her eyes acquired a feral look. Untying the belt of the robe, she stepped to the foot of the bed, facing him. She let the robe drop open and instantly the narrow column of light brown pubic became visible. Slowly she slipped the robe off her shoulders and dropped it across the bed.

Her form was, he thought, a classic hourglass, with a narrow waist and the top and bottom symmetrically proportioned. Her breasts, not large, were round and crowned with the lightest pink nipples, nipples whose erectness revealed her arousal.

Beth watched Jasper as he studied her form, obviously wanting him to say something about her appearance. "I think I look okay." Her voice had dropped to a whisper.

"No." He rose slowly, instantly aware of his thickening member, and took a step toward her. "You are not 'okay.' You are exquisite."

He reached for her shoulders and leaned forward to kiss her and she responded by putting her hands behind his head and forcing their mouths together, her tongue sliding into his mouth. His eyes closed, he felt the length of her naked body against him.

She held the kiss for only a moment, then pushed him back with hand and gripped his necktie. She yanked on it, jerking it from side to side as she tried to undo it.

"Damn!" she muttered. "All these months I've been waiting and now it's like I can't wait another minute."

"Let me help," he said.

He loosened his tie and whipped it out of his shirt collar, dropping it on the floor. By the time he had done that, she had undone his belt and unclasped and unzipped his pants. As his trousers tumbled to his knees, she twirled him toward the bed and pushed him backwards. When he stopped bouncing, they looked at each other and giggled.

A girlish smile crossed her face. "This is fun."

"Yes it is." He used his elbows to push himself toward the center of the bed. "Might be a whole lot of fun," he said as he began unbuttoning his shirt.

Now it was her voice that was girlish. "Let me help myself."

By the time he had pulled off his shirt and tossed it in the general direction of his tie, she had yanked off his shoes and socks and pants. She stood above him, gazing at the outline of his erect penis beneath his underwear. She leaned forward deliberately, put a hand on each of his hips and slid his underwear down his legs and off his feet.

Staring as his enraged member, a single clear drop on the very tip of the glans, she said softly, "Now that is exquisite."

Her face dissolved into giggles and she dropped atop the bed, crawling up, dragging her peaking nipples across his skin, until her face was just above his. She lowered herself onto him and, because she was a few inches shorter than he, he felt the head of his penis press against her clitoris, just inside the parted lips of her labia. Jasper looped his arms beneath her shoulder blades, holding her against him. He realized she had closed her eyes when he heard her sigh.

"It is just so good to feel you, skin against skin. It's so good to be held," she whispered.

The aroma of her shampoo, not sweet but fresh and beguiling, came to his nose. She was, he realized, just as he had described her—a refined, classy woman.

"This holding," he said, ". . . yes, it's good. Do you think it's really all you wanted, Beth?"

She raised her head and looked at him. "Hell no. I want it all. . . . I want you all." She pulled her lips against her teeth. "Look, Jasper, when I had my last baby I had my tubes tied. So I can't get pregnant. Still, I brought along a condom. I don't know if you want to use it."

He smiled. "I'm what they call 'D-and-D free'."

"Ooo," she giggled, "me too. We have so much in common."

Raising his head to her, Jasper kissed her. This time it was less urgent, less hurried. He felt her relax against him. She was giving him, he realized, the gift of trust.

"So I want to ask you something, Beth." When their eyes met, he continued, "Will you tell me what you like? I mean, when we're making love, what do you really, really enjoy? I want to make sure that's what we do."

"Um." She propped herself on her elbows on his chest, their faces an inch apart. "I guess, just regular sex. Lots of different positions maybe?" A little flush of red painted her face. "Also . . ."

"Yes."

"Well, I really like to be kissed. You know? Down there?"

A slow, wry smile came to him. "Well I really like to kiss you all over. Especially 'down there'." He feigned a frown. "But we have to do something first. We have to test the headboard."

"What?"

"Yeah. The headboard of the bed. What if it's loose and we get wild in here and people walking down the hall hear the banging?"

She smiled. "Seriously?"

"Hey, we're like newlyweds in here. You never know how acrobatic it might get, but still we want our privacy." He slid his hand down her sides—to which she shivered in delight—to her hips. "It's simple. I'll show you."

He began to ease her forward, her body moving upward over his toward the head of the bed. About the time her pelvis came to be even with his collarbone and she felt his hands on her silky behind, she realized what he was doing. Her mouth dropped open as she put her hands on the headboard of the bed, her eyes watching in awe as he guided the lips of her vagina down to his mouth. The outer petals of her labia already glistened with moisture as ran his tongue against them.

She surged, as if struck by an electric spark. "Oh! . . . Oh."

At first, when he roughed his tongue against her clitoris, there was little flavor to the fluid drops. But as he forced his tongue deep into her passage, her flow increased and the texture and taste of it became rich and tart. His right hand found her breast, the areola a raised ring of bumps, and she arched her back. As he moved his tongue back and forth, Beth pressed her pubis against his face, moving up and back against his tongue. Jasper felt a growing urgency within her and slipped his free hand beneath her, gently probing until he found the open lips of her vagina and sliding his middle finger upward to the mound behind her clit. He stroked in unison with her movements, which suddenly became erratic. He felt the walls of her sex tighten and literally felt the little explosion of air before the cute farting sound.

"Oh. Oh," she whispered breathlessly, looking down at his face. "Is that okay? Is that disgusting?" Slowly the movement of her pelvis stopped and she moved her bottom back so she could see Jasper's entire face.

"Was that okay? What I just did?"

He smiled. "Hmm. I'm not really sure. I have to do it again to see if it's acceptable."

When he put his hands on her buttocks to push her back up against his mouth, she resisted. "No wait. It's too sensitive. It's too sensitive." As she stared down at him, an anxious smile lit her face and he realized how truly beautiful she was. "Oh, what the hell. Go ahead, Jasper."

He eased her bottom toward his face. "We're going to take our time, now, darling Beth."

"We are?"

"Yes. Your job is to not come."

Her eyes closed and her chin rolled upward as she felt his tongue against her protruding clitoris. "Will I get fired if I do? . . . 'Cause I'm not sure I can keep from it."

He pulled away for an instant to respond. "Well then, you might get really screwed."

"Oh." Her eyes still closed, she began to rock against his face again. "We can't have that. . . . But still. Actually that sounds pretty good. . . ."

Jasper could feel her climax coming once more. He put his hand on her breast, sliding the nipple between his fingers slowly. With his other hand he pressed her tailbone firmly down, which created the feeling in her that she could not escape his tongue stimulating her vagina. And she came again, this time the burst of air was more explosive. Jasper felt her flow against his chin and neck. Almost instantly her limbs grew flaccid. She moaned as she became dead weight upon him.

He scooted her until their faces were together and she lay on him without moving or speaking for several minutes. At length she began to kiss him—his lips, his neck, his chest. Beth put her head on his chest with a sigh.

"I don't know what to say," she whispered.

"How about, 'make me come some more'."

Their eyes met and she said, "I am so selfish. Taking care of me and not taking care of you. . . . Still, I would like some more. Can we come together, love?"

"Only one way to find out."

She slid to the side and looked down at his cock and ran her

60

fingers down the length of it slowly. Immediately it became bone hard.

"I got this," she said in her girlish voice.

She sat up and squatted on his thighs, the variegated lips of her vagina—wet and fiery pink—on full display. Looking down, she carefully guided the glans of his member into her passage, then lowered herself onto him, causing his cock to glide deeply, fully into her. Slowly at first, she rocked her behind forward and back, her eyes closed in the ecstasy of the feeling. For his part, Jasper only arched his back to make the penetration complete as she settled onto him with each forward motion.

He was surprised at the speed and degree of his arousal. It was the erotic sensuality of the woman, he thought, that bought him close to climax so quickly. And, just as he was about to come, Beth suddenly stopped moving. Their eyes met, hers filled with delight and surprise as once again her passage burped the now familiar, undeniable proof of her orgasm.

It filled him with maddening desire. He put his hands on her hips and thrust upward into her again and again and immediately there came his own fierce orgasm. He moaned, holding her tightly against him, his penis deep within her. Gradually he relaxed against the bed, one arm over his eyes. He felt her collapse upon him, their ragged breathing united.

At length she spoke. "Now that was the celebration I've been hoping for."

He sighed. "Are you going to tell your friends all about it?"

She giggled. "They'll know what happened when they see my face." She played with the sweaty hair on his neck. "What should I tell them when they want to get in touch with you?"

Jasper laughed. "What a nice compliment. . . . You can tell them that it would take a woman as sweet and beautiful and sensual as Miss Beth Durbin to get me this worked up. So I'm not sure I could perform like this for anyone else."

When she didn't respond, he moved his arm to look at her. She was smiling at him.

"You always seem to know the right thing to say, Jasper."

He put a hand on her cheek. "Everything I've said about you is true, Beth. You are so good. So lovely. . . . You deserve only good things."

"Well what about you? You deserve good things too. So, tell me exactly why it is you don't have a girl."

"We broke up at the end of the semester. She went in one direction to work for one hospitality company and I came to this place. It was mutual."

"Why wouldn't she follow you? Even if for nothing but the sex?"

He laughed. "I don't think she was that much into sex."

"Oh my god." She rolled onto her side, lying next to him, her body pressed against him. "Am I just a horny little pervert?" She sighed. "Speaking of horny, honey, how long can your stay with me tonight?"

Chapter Five

When he heard the clattering sound at the glass front doors, Jasper looked up. It took a moment before what he was seeing registered with him—a young woman was holding a medium size, hard shell suitcase and was stuck trying to get into the hotel.

Immediately he rushed from behind the counter across the lobby. He forced the door open with one hand and took the suitcase with the other.

"Allow me to help you, ma'am."

She gasped in relief and followed him into the lobby.

Standing before her, speaking to her had allowed Jasper to get a good look at her and to begin to grasp her situation. She was petite, in her late twenties, he thought, dressed as a businesswoman in a sleeveless navy dress. While her arms and bare legs revealed that she was quite fair, her face was flushed dark red with exertion. Evidently she had been carrying the suitcase for some distance and, even though it was 9:15 and the sun had been down for half an hour, it was still in the mid 90s outside. She had also been carrying a pair of high heels that matched her dress, with a dark purse dangling from a strap over one shoulder.

Jasper led her to an overstuffed chair close to the registration counter, set the suitcase on the floor and motioned for her to sit down. "Why don't you rest here, ma'am?"

She sat down wordlessly, seeming to be extremely appreciative, drawing deep, healing breaths. It gave him a chance to study her more closely. If she did not have the appearance of having wandered out of a sauna, Jasper thought, she would have been quite attractive. Her oval face was accented by a prominent, sharp nose, chiseled lips and extremely dark eyes. Equally chocolate brown was her hair, straight and cut to just beneath her jaw line and parted on one side.

"Welcome to the *Plaisir*, ma'am," he said in the same tone he would have used if she had walked in calmly and come straight to the counter. "How may I assist you?"

She sighed. "Well, you can tell me that, even though this is a Friday night in the French Quarter, you still have a room available."

"Ah." Jasper turned and went behind the counter. "Oddly enough, ma'am, we had a cancellation earlier and we do have an available room." He came back around to her with a clipboard and a paper reservation form. "It's a single, king size on the first floor. The rate is $75 a night. Is that acceptable?"

"Acceptable? It's a fucking miracle."

"Very good, ma'am," he responded emotionlessly. "Why don't you just sit here and fill out the paperwork while I take your charge card and run it for you."

She leaned back in the chair and pulled her purse into her lap. Instantly she produced a platinum card, handed it to Jasper and took the clipboard. He saw, as he ran the card through the charge machine, that the name on it was that of an accounting firm in Saint Petersburg, Florida. Theoretically, he had been taught, he should have asked her to verify her identity since her name wasn't on the card. The circumstances of her arrival, he decided, were all the verification he needed.

"Here you are, ma'am." He handed her the room key and the charge receipt. "You're in room 110, which is just down the main hallway to the right, the second door."

She dropped both of them into her purse. "So is it okay if, like, I just sit here for another minute?"

"Take all the time you'd like, ma'am. May I get you a complimentary bottle of cool water?"

"Oh, that would be awesome."

"Certainly."

As he walked to the little refrigerator that held the bottle water, he glanced at the clipboard in his hand. Her name was Martina Collins and her address was in Saint Petersburg. Why, he wondered, did she show up late on a Friday evening needing a hotel room on the spur of the moment?

She uncapped the water and took a long drink. Then she leaned back again, showing no sign of standing and heading toward her room.

Jasper motioned to a chair facing hers. "Do you mind if I sit here, Ms. Collins?"

"Ms. Collins?" The woman gave him an admiring little smile. "You're a quick read. Please, sit down." She sized him up as he sat down across from her. "You're Jaz?"

64

He smiled. "Jasper, ma'am. My colleagues here decided my name was not sufficiently worthy of New Orleans."

"Jaz is good," she said, taking another drink.

"Not to be intrusive, Ms. Collins, but I see your suitcase has wheels. Yet you were carrying it when you arrived."

"Yeah." She nodded. "That's why I'm so damn winded. I broke one of the wheels when I was leaving the Downstream."

He felt his eyebrows arch involuntarily. "The Downstream Hotel, ma'am, over on Market Street?"

"Yes. That's the one. This place is the third hotel I've walked to looking for a room—the first one with a vacancy. And I had to carry that freaking suitcase the whole way."

The Downstream Hotel and Resort was one of the most exclusive hospitality sites in the entire city. Jasper wondered why she would leave it on a Friday night with no other reservation and obviously no transportation.

"Well, we're glad you came to the *Plaisir*, Ms. Collins. May I ask, how many nights will you be with us?"

"Two nights. Tonight and Saturday. I catch the plane back to Saint Pete about noon Sunday."

Jasper nodded. "Very good. I'd like to offer some assistance if I might, ma'am. Once you get to your room and unpack, if you'll let us have your bag we have a gentleman who is quite skilled at dealing with such problems. He can replace the defective wheel and have your suitcase ready, like new, by the time you're ready to check out Sunday. Of course there is no charge for the repair. You can give the repairman a gratuity if you wish."

She gazed at him. "By god, that's a great deal. If you'll carry it to my room here in a minute or two, I'll dump everything out of it and you can have it now."

"Of course."

Even though her face was still flushed and she showed no sign of moving from the chair, the young woman seemed to be less winded. She also appeared to relax a bit and grow more comfortable. Turning the bottle up, she finished the water.

"So." She looked at Jasper. "Want to know how I broke the wheel on my suitcase, and why I left the Downstream in a big, fat hurry?"

He tried to appear attentive without being overly curious—

which he definitely was. "Why is that, Ms. Collins?"

"My boyfriend's wife showed up."

". . . I take it that was a surprise?"

She nodded slowly. "I guess he's not really my boyfriend. He's more like my boss."

"I see."

"I've been telling Jerry the last couple weeks that his wife was getting suspicious. She was dropping by the office at odd times and calling him on the business phone repeatedly during the day. Jerry says, 'Well, I'll set up a weekend business trip to New Orleans. She can be as suspicious as she wants from 1500 miles away.'"

"Yes, ma'am."

"So we checked into the Downstream and went out for supper and had just gotten back to the room by maybe fifteen or twenty minutes when the phone in the room rings. I answer it. It's the concierge. He says, 'Please tell Mr. Downs that we gave the second room key to his wife. She just got onto the elevator.'"

Jasper recognized immediately the "early warning" the Downstream concierge had given the lovers. He would remember that lesson, he thought, for coming times when he was in that position.

"Well, we were on the tenth floor on the back hallway. I had just time enough to put on the clothes I had taken off, grab my stuff and shoot out the door. On my way out, Jerry says to me, 'Take the stairs. Use the business card. I'll see you Sunday on the plane unless I text you with a different plan.'"

"Yes, ma'am."

She drew a deep breath. "I couldn't get into that stairwell and down the first flight fast enough. And on that first flight, I was pulling my suitcase and it banged onto the marble steps and broke the wheel." She shook her head. "I had to carry the damn thing down nine floors and for however many miles it took to get here."

"Well," Jasper replied, "you won't be carrying it anymore. We'll fix it like new before you leave."

She tilted her head and looked at him. "Isn't it a little unusual for a place like this to have a concierge? I mean, I wasn't surprised at the service we got at the Downstream. But the 'High Pleasure Hotel'? I mean it as a compliment when I say you're a little more than I was expecting."

Jasper smiled. "Thank you, Ms. Collins. Well, as long as we're . . . sharing stories, I am a senior hospitality major from Idaho Tech. There is an international program that allows apprenticeships for those who want to become a concierge. A hospitality establishment pays half the salary of an apprentice and the program pays the other half. The *Plaisir* heard about it and saw it as a great way to get a night manager for the summer at half price."

She grinned. "So we were both lured to New Orleans under false pretenses to get screwed."

Jasper laughed. He couldn't help himself. Her intelligence expressed itself in a marvelous quick wit.

"I suppose you could say that, yes, ma'am. In your case, you get to go home on Sunday. I've got two more weeks before I'm free from the farce, so to speak. And, when I get back to Idaho, just as if I had been in the program at an exclusive establishment like the Downstream, I can put on my credentials that I completed the concierge program."

A slow, wry smile crossed her face. "So you are the concierge apprentice. Sort of like 'The Sorcerer's Apprentice.'"

He returned her smile. "Without the music or the magic, I'm afraid."

She straightened. She seemed about ready to get up and go to her room. "Well, I'm forever grateful to that concierge who called our room while ago." She stood. "Otherwise I would have been carrying this stupid suitcase looking for a job as well as a hotel."

"Allow me, ma'am."

Jasper lifted the suitcase by the handle and started down the hallway toward room 110. The woman followed him wordlessly. The suitcase wasn't overly heavy, he thought, but carrying it down nine flights of stairs and through the streets of the French Quarter in the heat and humidity would wear anyone out.

He turned to her when they stood in front of the door and held out his hand for the key. Opening the door, he stepped back and let her enter. She stood in the center of the room, looking around, clearly surprised and pleased.

"This isn't bad at all." She glanced at him. "Just put the suitcase on the bed, if you will."

She came to his side and opened the suitcase immediately, unceremoniously taking out the great variety of clothes inside. He was somewhat amazed at all she had brought for a three-day trip. There were at least three sexy nightgowns and a skimpy bathing suit—the Downstream, he remembered, had the large indoor pool—plus an evening gown and several short outfits. She seemed unabashed to be revealing all her clothes to him. It brought to his mind the statement one of his hospitality professors had made, that a concierge was like a cabdriver or waiter: "You know you're doing your job properly when you are completely ignored."

"Well, here's this." She latched the suitcase and handed it to him.

"Thank you, Ms. Collins. We'll have it for you at the front desk when you're ready for it. Ring and we'll bring it to your room."

She turned backwards and flopped across the bed. "I have no doubt, Jaz." She put her hands behind her head. Lying there, looking up at him, she smiled. "My name is Marti."

"Yes, ma'am."

"I really, truly appreciate this."

"We are delighted you are here, Marti Collins. In the interest of full disclosure, the couple who had reserved this room didn't really cancel. They actually got in a huge argument in the lobby when they were checking in. The wife told the husband she wasn't interested in reconciling, that she was ready to go through with the divorce and then stormed out. Not long after that he just sort of wandered out as well." He shrugged. "Since they never made it back to the room, it remained in its pristine condition without any intervention from housekeeping."

"Just out of curiosity, what were they fighting about."

"The price of the room."

"Seriously? Seventy-five bucks a night?"

"Well, no ma'am. The rate is actually $115. With tax it's over $125. While that's actually pretty low for New Orleans on a seasonal weekend, the wife thought it was extravagant."

She studied his face. "How did I get it for $75?"

Jasper shrugged. "You seemed to be in a certain amount of distress. I just used the concierge's discretion."

"So . . . how far does your concierge service extend?"

He expression was emotionless. "As far as necessary, ma'am."

"Well okay, junior sorcerer. Right now I'm pretty much exhausted and I can't wait to get a good night's sleep. But tomorrow

I'm stuck in a city I know nothing about. What are the chances you could be my guide tomorrow? You can show me around and I can feed you like a king—since I got the business credit card. And I'm not afraid to use it."

He nodded slowly. "I think that would be a whole lot of fun. Marti."

She smiled, a mischievous, naughty smile. "Will you be up in time for lunch?"

"Of course. And I'm off tomorrow evening."

"Wow. Excellent. So what if we meet in the lobby at noon?"

"I look forward to that more than I can say."

Jasper came down to the lobby half an hour early on Saturday only to find Marti was already waiting for him. She wore a dark purple, sleeveless short outfit that revealed and highlighted a lot more of her feminine charms than her simple dress had the night before. It made him understand why Jerry Downs was so interested in her. And why Mrs. Downs was so jealous and suspicious.

The instant she saw him she hopped up from the same chair she had been sitting in the night before and took his hand in hers. When she did, Jasper noticed that she had painted her fingernails to match her purple outfit. He also observed, from the corner of his eye, that Flo and Tizzy were watching—their mouths open—as Marti walked beside him, hands swinging, out the front door into the French Quarter.

They began their excursion with shrimp po' boys and sweet tea for lunch and a carriage ride around the Quarter, followed by a walking tour of the street artists. They made the long trek both ways down Market Street through the commercial souvenir shops and then the handmade local goods vendors. Periodically they were separated by a few feet as she studied trinkets and baubles, giving him an opportunity to watch the movements of her perfectly shaped behind as she walked and bent over and straightened up.

Afterwards came a slow stroll down Bourbon Street, with Marti firmly hanging onto his hand as they gazed at the nude clubs and tough saloons. Jasper shared a certain amount of running dialogue about the history and social significance of the places they were seeing, in the process surprising himself with how much he had learned about Nola in the two months he had been there.

At one point, Jasper realized they were within a block of the Downstream and asked, "Marti, do you realize how close we are to your boss's hotel? Are you concerned that we might bump into them?"

"Ha! Not in a million years. Once Clarice showed up, he had to perpetrate that this was an actual business trip, meaning he had to leave her all day in the hotel while he went off somewhere and pretended to be in meetings. He can't drink or party at all, because he has to come back looking, smelling and acting like he's been around a bunch of CPAs. And poor Clarice would be way too scared to venture out into the city by herself." She glanced at him. "Yeah, he may have kicked me out last night, but I'm the one enjoying the trip."

He smiled. "I'm glad of that. You aren't tired of walking?"

"I don't mind walking at all, as long as I'm not carrying a thirty-five pound suitcase." She watched a woman, wearing sharp casual clothes, pass them. "So I have a question, Jaz."

"What's that?"

"I get the couples we see and I get the street walkers, but who are these grown-ass women my mom's age walking down Bourbon Street by themselves?"

He shrugged. "Well, people come here to hook up. Male, female, young, old, straight, gay—Nola is the place to get laid."

She nodded slowly. "I guess I lucked out," she said quietly, leaving him to wonder what she meant.

They could hear a street concert near the Mississippi levy and walked toward the river past mimes, statue men with boom boxes and outstretched hands, buskers with brass instruments playing jazz, and street vendors.

There was a ten-year-old black girl dressed as Michael Jackson standing motionless beside a huge radio, her pork pie hat outstretched in her hand. Entranced, Marti opened her purse and dropped a dollar into the hat. Instantly the child pushed a button with her toe and "Billie Jean" began to play loudly. The girl's herky-jerky movements were amazing like those of Jackson. Marti watched, her mouth open, as the song ran its course. The instant it ended, the girl toed the music box and froze in place. Marti clapped. She whispered something in the girl's ear and dropped another dollar into the re-extended hat.

When she bent over to speak to the girl, Marti's loose top once again revealed to Jasper a tantalizing view of her braless breasts, creamy pale and dark-nippled and perfectly proportioned. He couldn't push the thought of them out of his mind. As they walked back down Market Street, he considered what other, nearby sites might interest her.

"Not far from here," he said, "is a wonderful praline and chocolate place, if you like that. They give free samples. Then, when you get ready for supper, I'd like to take you to a café on the square that serves fresh redfish from Lake Pontchartrain. They also have, you know, steaks and chicken if you prefer."

She looked at him casually. "I'll tell you what I prefer. Just how far are we from our hotel?"

"The *Plaisir*? Not far at all. Maybe, uh, four or five blocks. Are you ready to go back?"

"For a while, maybe." She stopped Jasper without dropping his hand and stood before him, looking up at him. "Here's the deal. The longer we've been walking, the hornier I've gotten until, right now, it's hard to think of anything else. So what I really want—if you're interested and you're game—is for you to take me back to my room and fuck my brains out."

He stared at her. "Well, Marti Collins . . . I would be delighted to give it my best shot. Or three or four of my best shots."

She smiled broadly. "Let's not run. We don't want to waste our strength. But do let us be in a hurry."

He began to lead her back to the hotel. The closer they got and the more she realized where was and how close the hotel was, the more she took the lead. When it got to the point she was pretty much pulling him along, Jasper felt himself begin to smile.

"Just so you know," she said, "I have an IUD."

"Yeah? I've always wanted to taste one of those."

She laughed and glanced at him. "You look pretty clean, Jaz. Should we use protection?"

"If you think you should. I am drug and disease free though."

"Then let's go *au natural*. Here," she said, as they jaywalked across the street toward the hotel, "we should go through the side entrance here, so it doesn't cause you any trouble with the people you work for."

He laughed. "Funny that you would say that. The manager's mistress used to be the night clerk. When I showed up, it gave them the chance to spend their evenings together."

Marti opened the door to the north hallway without letting go of Jasper and went straight to her room. She pressed her key into his hand with her back to the door so he had to reach around her to open it. As he did, she began to unbutton his shirt and pull it from his jeans. He smiled broadly, trying to decide if she was distracting him from opening the latch or opening the latch was distracting him from her. When she heard the door open, she slid her fingers inside his pants, turned and pulled him into the room.

She waved an arm as if she were showing him something. "This is my room." She kissed him hard and pulled him down onto the bed on his side facing her. "And this is my fucking bed."

"That is my intention," he replied softly.

Marti sat up and pulled her purple top over her head without unbuttoning it, her wonderfully mobile breasts jiggling gloriously. She lay flat on her back and slid her shorts and panties off in one smooth motion. Jasper stared at her completely shaved pudendum and her small, oval vagina.

She gave him an indignant look. "Don't you have some skin to show me, boy?"

Smiling, he got to his feet, kicked off his shoes and stepped out of his pants and underwear. He heard her draw a breath. She reached out and gently grasped his thickening member.

"Oh," she said softly, "why did I waste this day walking around New Orleans?" As she pulled on his cock, it grew stiff almost instantly beneath her intense gaze. "So, I have to ask you, how long can you fuck until you come?"

Studying her marvelous, porcelain form, he said, "Well, that depends. You already have me really aroused. So I'm not sure. The good news is, I recover really well in five or ten minutes."

"Hot damn. Okay. Then we have to start with sixty-nine first, if you don't want to taste your jizz."

Using his engorged member like a joystick, she guided him skillfully onto the bed and onto his back and immediately straddled him upside down. He felt her mouth descend onto his penis, stimulating him without overly exciting him. Marti knew, he realized, exactly what she was doing.

At the same time her small, open vagina appeared before his face. Jasper captured her behind in his hands and admired what he saw for a few seconds before guiding her labia to his lips. He pressed his tongue against her clitoris and sucked it against his teeth. She squirmed and responded by sucking as much of his cock into her mouth as she could. He slid his tongue deeply into her vagina and gently ran a finger back and forth onto her clit and then farther it. When he felt Marti respond by leaning down onto his face, he continued. Focusing on her response to his stimulation helped him ignore the maddening blow job she was giving him. After several minutes, she stopped, taking his dick from her mouth and lying against him heavily. The flavor of her poon changed from waxy to acidic, her limbs became flaccid and suddenly she began to quiver. A jolt ran through her as if something had struck her, then again and again. She moaned each time and collapsed limply atop him.

When she did not move or speak for several seconds, Jasper wondered if she had experienced *le petit mort,* the orgasm that renders women unconscious. Then he heard her voice.

"Fuck me now, Jaz."

When he rolled her onto her back, despite her eyes being closed he saw that she wore a tranquil smile. She arched her back and spread her legs. Jasper sat on his knees, his back straight and pulled her toward him, his cock—slick with precum and her saliva—slid into her vagina. She sighed.

As he held her legs apart, around his hips and rocked forward, his penis bumped and stopped with each forward thrust. Her passage, he realized, was not only small but shallow.

Marti opened her eyes. "Oh, Jaz. Am I low-bridging you, honey. Let me fix that."

She disengaged from him and rolled onto her side, raising her upper leg and keeping her lower leg straight. She moved him expertly so that his knees were on either side of her lower leg and raised her behind slightly off the bed so he could see the pink and purple opening of her labia.

"Try it now."

This time his cock slid slowly, fully in. An expression of ecstasy on her face, she closed her eyes. Her back arched.

As he moved forward and back, keeping his thrusts slow and measured and trying not to become too excited, he felt the woman's body respond to his. She tightened her legs against him and gradually changed the position on the bed—to maximize the feeling of his penis within her. Then, over several minutes, he felt the inner walls of her vagina thicken while, as before, her body fell limp. Again she moaned as if in agony and the spasms seized her, this time seeming more severe than before. If she had not been experiencing climax, Jasper would have been alarmed. He slowed his motion and stopped, gazing down at her with a smile.

"Did you come?" she asked without opening her eyes.

"Not yet."

"Then why the fuck did you stop?"

Instantly he was excruciatingly aroused and Jasper thrust fully into her. Though she was like a rag doll—her arms, head and chest seeming to have no power of their own—her legs were taut against him. Leaning down, he propped his body with one hand without slowing his motion and with the other hand he manipulated one tantalizing, sweet breast with its nipple peaking between his finger. She jumped as if shocked and emitted one long slow moan, ending in another climax—this one marked by her own rapid, unison movements onto and away from his cock. That was all Jasper could take. He surged into her again and again, and came explosively.

"Ah. Ah. Ah." He heard his own breathing and felt the throbbing of his penis as he continued to release within her. "Ah. Ah. . . . Marti . . ."

There was joy and mockery in her voice. ". . . Jasper."

As the electric thrill of the climax passed, he fell onto his side, spooning her. He pulled her against him, his still-enlarged penis teased by the sweet roundness of her behind. Wetness—his and hers—spilled from her onto his bottom thigh and onto the bed. As they lay silently, their breathing gradually calming, he felt her nipples, pressed against his inner arm, loses their tautness. He closed his eyes and kissed the back of her neck, her shoulders and down her spine.

Softly she spoke, "I'm so fortunate. I'm lucky Jerry kicked me out. Lucky that those other hotels didn't have a vacancy. Lucky that you were here. Lucky that you have the cock of my dreams."

He gave a breathless laugh. "So, not to bring up a sore subject, but do you think your boss and his wife are having the kind of wonderful sex we're having?"

"Ha." She rolled onto her back and then to her side to face him. "I can assure you they are not." She ran her fingers across his cheek slowly. "So I've made love to Jerry probably . . . I don't know, six or eight times. He's never made me climax. . . . Now you, on the other hand, made me come three times. So far. And once without even sticking a dick in me."

Jasper grinned. "I think you just gave me a compliment. Thank you. . . . Well, what would you do then if your boss, after this near-disaster, decided he loved you more than he loves his wife and decided to leave her and ask you to marry him?"

Marti laughed aloud. She shook her head. "Not in a million years."

"Really?"

"For at least four good reasons." She leaned forward and kissed him. "For starters, he's almost old enough to be my dad, but he's not near rich enough to be a sugar daddy—if I wanted one, which I don't. Second, he doesn't arouse me. I cannot imagine being married to a guy who doesn't turn me on and can't make me come. Third, I've passed all my CPA tests except for one and I'm going to pass it in the next couple months and get a job back where I'm from in Maryland. Or maybe I'll go to Delaware. They're always looking for willing accountants."

He laughed "'Willing accountants'? What's that?"

She smiled sweetly. "Don't you know? The last question they ask an accountant before offering her the job is, 'What does 2 plus 2 equal?' And the correct answer is, 'What do you want it to equal?'"

"I see. I had no idea being an accountant had so much in common with being a concierge."

"Yep. And reason number four: Jerry is going to give me a killer recommendation."

"Do tell?"

"Yes. I plan on telling him exactly what I want him to say. And if he has a problem with that, his wife will tell him exactly what I want him to say."

"Ah. Isn't that sort of blackmail? Or, since you're an accountant, I guess it would be extortion."

"Well, which is worse, putting the screws to the boss for a good reference—which I deserve by the way; I am a really good accountant—or putting your pecker in the payrolls? There are ethical constraints and laws against that too, you know."

"Oh yes." He propped his elbow on the bed and his head in his hand. "In the concierge program we pledge to maintain a strict code of ethical behavior, including no sexual contact with clients."

"Really? Well I'm glad you turned out to be more practical than ethical."

"That and this really isn't a legit concierge program. Making love to a smoking hot guest is my revenge on the duplicity of the High Pleasure Hotel."

She giggled and her breasts danced. "Well, what about you, Jaz. Surely have a girl, don't you?"

"No. I had a girl I dated the last couple years, but she and I decided to break it off since we were headed in different directions."

"No, I mean here. If you've been here this whole summer, surely you've got a girl or six you've been seeing."

He shook his head. "Honestly, no. There just aren't many available girls my age I see who aren't passing through, spending a few days here in Nola. It's not like college where you break up with somebody one day and meet somebody else the next."

"Still, you must have met some girls. What about that cute little hottie I saw this morning serving breakfast? The one in blue jeans with the tight tank top and the killer tits? She's Spanish I think."

"Oh, that's Flo. She's Cajun, not Spanish."

"A Cajun named 'Flo'?"

"Her name is Fleur Printemps, but nobody around here can say it right. Yes, she is extremely attractive—I hope I can say that without offending present company."

"Of course. I recognize a fuckable woman when I see one."

He chuckled. "Well, alluring as she is, Flo is strictly off limits."

"Oh? Says who? She wasn't wearing a ring."

"Says her Cajun boyfriend, Anton."

"Anton?"

"Yes, 'Anton, slayer of the horny'."

"Oh. . . . That's too bad, Jaz."

"You're telling me."

". . . I have an idea."

"Oh? I like your ideas"

"Let's take a shower together. Then we'll go have redfish. Then we'll come back here and fuck our brains out."

He nodded slowly. "You're so smart and creative."

"Yeah? Well if this concierge gig doesn't work out, you could be a gigolo."

Chapter Six

The sound of his door unlatching and opening woke Jasper. Disoriented and confused, he sat up in the bed, bare chested, sheets covering him to his waist.

The door opened fully and Flo came, her bearing completely casual. "Good morning, Jaz boy."

"Flo." He squeezed his eyes shut and shook his head. "Did I oversleep? What time is it?"

"Just after noon. Rise with a shine."

"Flo, go away." He slid back down on the sheets. "I don't get up for another three or four hours."

She sat on the foot of his bed, undeterred. "Welcome to this, you last week in Nola, bro. This time next Monday, you be on the plane to Iowa."

"Idaho, girlie. Did you think I'd lost track of the days? I know I got five more shifts and then I'm done."

"Oh, Jaz boy, you make me think maybe you don't be liking Nola."

He rolled toward her and propped himself up on one elbow. "I like New Orleans. I enjoy the city and the Quarter. I like the food and the craziness. There isn't much I don't like about it except this hotel and the way I got tricked into working here."

Her face folded into a faux frown. "You don't like the work with me?"

"I got nothing against you and Manuel. You two work hard and you keep the hotel functioning and making a profit, despite Sol's best efforts. You, in particular, are smart a hell and totally wasted on the *Plaisir*. And I got nothing against Tizzy except she's incompetent. I don't have that much against Sol, except that he's a con artist and he fooled me into losing a whole summer when I should've been learning to be a concierge."

"You don't think you learn a whole lot?"

He shook his head. "What did I learn exactly? I already knew how to check people in and out of a hotel. I knew how to run a cash register and carry suitcases."

"*Oui*, and when you came you knowed already how to be a snot-nose, pretend to be too-cool-for-the-school, eh?"

He stared at her. Was this why she had come into his room for the first time all summer and awakened him? Was this last week going to be a time of torment? Were Flo and perhaps everyone else on the staff intentionally going to give him grief about his attitude? He had strived not to put on airs, not to look down on them or to remind them constantly that he had been deceived into taking the night manager position.

"Look, Flo, if I came across as condescending, I apologize. I promised you the first day that I would be professional in all my relationships with the staff. If I failed in that, I'm sorry. Frankly I didn't realize I had acted badly. It would have been good for you to point that out to me. I would have corrected it."

She considered his words. "What is that 'con-si-dencing.'"

"Uh," he tried to keep any patronizing tone from his voice, "it's 'condescending.' It means acting as if you think your better than someone."

"Oh. Well you never did that to me or nobody."

He sat up and gazed at her, full of curiosity. Why was she in his room? After a full summer, had she suddenly decided to become playful and contrary?

"Quite the opposed, I should tell you," she said with a supremely casual expression. "I guess it okay to tell you from me now what a very good job you do. Too late for you to make the head big."

"Big head about what?"

"Reviews," she said, as if he should already have known what she was talking about. "I do the online, you know."

"Yeah?"

"Well, since you be the night guy, our reviews a whole lot better. 'Specially the 'quality of service.' You get some lot of comments too, boy. People say some nice things about our concierge."

He leaned back, propped up by the headboard. ". . . I'll be damned."

"So." Flo shrugged. "Manuel and me be sorry to see you go back to Iowa."

"If I was going to Iowa I might be sorry too, Flo. I'm going to Idaho. . . . And thanks for telling me all that. Do you suppose you could forward those comments to me? Along with any negative ones, of course."

"Negative like the bad?" She shook her head. "Nobody have no bad to say 'bout you, Jaz man."

He smiled ruefully. "Well. It wasn't a total loss."

She stretched her shoulders and arched her back and Jasper averted his eyes from her voluptuous breasts, concealed as always beneath the sheer white blouse and white stretch top. Their eyes met and he was surprised to see she was smiling. She kicked off her tennis shoes, stood and climbed onto the king-sized bed, sitting next to him, her back to the headboard.

He had felt uncertain, but now felt alarmed, as if he were being tested or trapped.

"So, Jaz, you get to do everything you wanted this summer in Nola?"

He eyed her suspiciously. "On my salary? I got to do everything that was free. I saw lots of cool sights. Of course I learned a lot of stuff the tourists wouldn't learn in a million years."

Flo put her hands behind her head as she listened, not looking at him, then responded, "What about, did you get to do everyone you wanted to?"

Jasper assumed he had misunderstood her. "Did I what?"

"Did you *faire l'amour* all the fine ladies you wanted to?"

". . . Fair . . ."

"Make the love, stupid boy. Did you take to bed all the ones you wanted?"

He laughed. "Why are you giving me shit, Flo? Is this in honor of it being my last week?"

She wasn't looking at him as she began to speak. "So . . . there was the pretty blonde Texas lady. She come to Nola looking for some and she sure found it, eh?"

His chest tightened suddenly. Did she know something or was she just guessing? Why had she singled out Beth Durbin?

"Before that was one of the cheerleaders who don't want to get drunk and high with the others." She slapped her hand against the mattress. "You do her right here in this very bed, Jaz."

That was Mattie Lewis. He wanted to correct her and say they were sorority sisters, not cheerleaders, but Flo would perceive that as an admission she was right.

"Now let's see. What about that tall, naughty woman—old as your mom—who like to make love naked with the curtain open. Kinky like hell, I bet she was."

He shook his head, remembering Lorraine Baxter, her bare behind protruding toward him and her hands on the window in the darkened room. "Where do you—"

"And Friday before last, that *petite fille* from Florida wearing the purple." Flo turned to him and smiled. "You left out of here holding her hand, but you come back and held everything she got, no?"

Clearly she knew what he had done and who he had done it with. How did she know and what did she intend to do with the knowledge?

"I'm not saying there is any validity to—"

"'Val-i-day-ty?'"

"Validity. It means truth. I'm not saying that I had anything to do with any of those ladies you mentioned. For the sake of argument, though, let me ask two questions. How would you know something like that and why would you tell me about it now?"

She turned her gaze from him to her bare toes, moving back and forth. Quietly she said, "I know because I heard you."

". . . What?"

Flo nodded. "You know I do the online and all the tech for—"

"Yes, I know that. What's that got to do with anything?"

She pointed to the house phone on his nightstand. "The new phone system. I set up so I can listen to what's happening in any room in the *Plaisir*."

Jasper's jaw dropped. "You listen to what's happening in the guests' rooms? In my room? . . . For Christ's sake, do you listen every night?"

"No, no, no, no. I only listen when you fucking."

He stared at her, struggling to understand. "How would you know?"

"Manny told me. Mostly."

". . . Manuel told you when I was making love to women?"

"He don't listen. He don't even know I can listen. I just asked him to tell me when you go to the room of a lady by yo'self."

He gazed at her, uncertain if he were more alarmed or curious. ". . . Why? Why would you do that."

For the first time she seemed a little unsure of herself. She shrugged sheepishly. "I want to know about you. I could toll you was different kind of fellow, even though you look me over pretty good. I decide to investigate the Jaz man. To see how you was with the ladies, you know. So I toll Manny to tell me when you went to see a lady by yo'self. And I listen in, you know. But with the cheerleader, I figure out myself she might be here with you after what you said about them girls. And, the little purple one? I watch all day to see when you bring her back to her room."

". . . Oh my god," he said slowly.

"And you so respectful. You so decent and listen so good to them. Never force yo'self on them. With the Texas lady, you even ask if she really want you lumber, or just for you to hold her. Oh, I mean, you fuck like the rabbit when you get the start. And I don't hear no complaints from no lady when you making that love. Except maybe they run out of time to spend with you and they want some more. Seem like they always want more."

He vacillated between feeling violated and complimented. Still, he wondered, if she were just into being a voyeur, why was she revealing it now?

". . . So, you're telling me this, like, as an apology?"

"Oh hell no. Ain't no regret I have for listening. You always amazing. I listen with my vibrator on, you know."

"What?"

"And you know that girl last Friday? When she check out and waiting for the taxi on Sunday, I stand by her side all normal and I ask, 'If you don't mind my ask, was you with the Jaz man in the bed?' 'Course I knowed she was. But she admit it. You slept with her all the night Saturday. So then, I ask her, 'How was the man?'" She smiled broadly. "And she toll me."

Jasper shook his head and buried his face in his hands. "Well, since you are obviously not apologizing for spying on me, why are you telling me this?"

Flo's face took on a totally different expression. For the first time in all the weeks he had known her, worked with her and been around her, she seemed vulnerable, tender. She pulled her knees to her chest before she answered.

"You say something about me when you with the little woman. You say you attracted to me. You said other very nice things. . . .

81

You even know my name and how to say it right, Fleur Printemps."

". . . Well, she asked about you. I was just being honest."

She nodded. "That's it in the shell of the nut, Jaz man. No greater compliment than for a man to be with a beautiful woman— just *faire l'amour* with that woman—and talk about how much he like a different woman. Me."

Without another word, she slipped off the sheer white blouse and tossed it to the foot of the bed.

"What are doing?" he asked.

Flo undid the clasp of her jeans. She raised her hips and slid her pants down and pulled them off her ankles, leaving her with nothing on but the stretch top and silky, white panties. And as she did, Jasper hopped out of the bed and stood staring at her in anxious disbelief. For her part, Flo was transfixed by the outline of his penis within his underwear, the only clothes he wore.

"Oh my god, you already got the hard on?"

"No." He looked down. "It's not hard and it's not going to get hard."

"If that's what it is before, what's it like when it's all the way? I can make him a bone."

"No, Flo! Stop. Just stop. I don't know what you're doing or why, but I told you when I first got here that I was going to be professional with you. Completely. And you told me about Anton, which I didn't forget."

He tried to relax and focus on what he was saying and forget he was standing in front of this delightful, alluring woman just in his underwear and that his dick in fact was getting a little hard. He could feel a little drop of pre cum which was sure to saturate through the gray fabric and become visible.

"When I was in high school," he said, "I almost got in a fight with a guy over a girl. We had been friends before, but we were about to duke it out and the girl was standing right there watching us. Just before I punched his lights out, the girl says, 'You guys aren't going to fight over me, are you?' . . . Right then I realized something. She had told me she loved me. She had told my friend she loved him. But really the only thing she was in love with was the idea that two boys were going to have a fist fight over her. . . . So I said to the other guy right then, 'Take her. I'm not interested in her.'"

"And you tell me this because of Anton?"

"Of course. Did the two of you break up or something?"

"You and me right now has nothing to do with Anton."

"It has everything to do with Anton. As much as you have talked about him all summer—even in the last couple weeks—it couldn't just end between you two like that. There has to be some drama involved here. Maybe you had a fight or maybe you broke up or maybe you think it's over between you, but that doesn't mean he thinks it's over. The way you've described the guy, he sounds a little possessive."

She gave him a little grin. "This have nothing to do with Anton."

"How can you say that?"

"'Cause ain't no Anton."

". . . What?"

"Anton, I imagine he a figment."

". . . Are you saying Anton is nothing but a figment of your imagination?"

"*Oui*, Jaz man. Only you can know this. Nobody else, include Sol."

A wry smile emerged and spread slowly across his face. "You invented Anton to keep people like me from coming onto you."

She nodded. "Make-believe Anton work too. Sol patted me only once on the ass and then I tell him Anton don't like that and never again Sol touch me."

They stared at each other. At last almost everything between them had been disclosed.

Flo fluffed the covers and pulled the sheet up to her neck. He watched as she wiggled beneath them and tossed out in succession the white top and then her panties. She lay on her side, smiling at him.

"You want to see more. You got to show more," she said.

Wordlessly he slid his shorts down his legs and stepped out of them. He stood motionless and half erect, watching for her reaction.

"*Oh mon dieu*," she said quietly. One arm came out from under the sheets, the hand outstretched toward him. "Bring him to me. Bring the man to me."

Jasper dropped onto his bed. He, lifted the sheet and admired the naked form he had longed for all summer, the spherical breasts with circular areolas and shocking pink nipples; the dark triangle of thick pubic hair above the stem of a clitoris and the curved line of her vagina.

Fleur took on an expression of urgency as she slid onto her back and pulled him on top of her. "So, now fuck me, Jaz."

"Isn't it a little soon? I mean aren't you—"

"*J'ai été* wet when I walk through the door. Fuck me."

She enveloped his hips with her legs and he guided his member to the lips of her passage. Jasper was surprised to find them quite slick. She pulled him down to her and into her and sighed. For an instant they lay knotted, their eyes closed, motionless, euphoric with their shared, deep embrace. Then she whispered to him.

"Fuck me."

Slowly he began to move up and back, his cock seemed amazingly rigid and massive to him, sliding forth fully through the moist lips and down. Then suddenly, startling him, only a minute after they began to make love, she began to come. She writhed against him madly, rocking back and forth against his member as he tried to maintain his steady thrusts and tried to avoid his own climax that he felt beginning to stir.

"Ahhh. Ahhh. . . . Jaz." She dug her fingers into the back of his shoulders. "Ah. . . . Jaz." She relaxed against the bed, opening her eyes and looking at him.

Jasper continued to sex her, moving fully but gently forward and back, his eyes locked on hers.

"I waiting all summer for that coming," she said quietly. Her expression became urgent. "And for this one here."

She turned her head to the side and pressed her pelvis upward to maximize the feeling of his penis entering. Jasper recognized he couldn't hold his own orgasm at bay any longer and his thrusting became pounding. He too began to moan.

This time they climaxed together, fiercely, his member extended fully within her and her pushing up against him, then moving up and back feverishly until she collapsed against the bed and he leaned his weight upon her, his cock still within her, her legs around him.

When her breathing began to slow, she said, "Purple girl say right."

". . . Marti Collins? What about her?"

"She toll me, if I didn't take you to bed, I really missing out. . . . Bro, she was so right." She drew a breath and said. "For sure you going to need the clean sheets, Jaz."

"As long as you're going to change them, we might as well mess them up good," he said.

She giggled. "You got time? Oh! I almost forgot. You ain't got time."

"What?"

"What the time?"

"Uh." He glanced at the clock radio on his nightstand. "About 12:45. Why?"

"That's why I came early to you."

She rolled him onto his back and climbed atop him, their faces inches apart. Putting her hands behind his head, she kissed him, holding their mouths together. Her tongue searched inside his mouth. She lifted her head and took a breath and kissed him again.

"First I ask you," she said. "Every day this week, can I come wake up you—and you lumber—at 3 or 4?"

"Uh, yeah. That works for me." He smiled, putting his hands behind his head lazily and enjoyed the feel of her wet nakedness against him.

"So today I came early because there someplace you got to go at 2."

"Somewhere I have to be at 2?"

"*Oui.*"

"And where might that be?"

"The big ass hotel, you know. Down the River."

"The Downstream?"

"Yeah, that it."

"Why do I have to go there?"

"You have to take the valuation papers for concierge."

He gazed at her. ". . . I have to take my concierge evaluation to the Downstream?"

"I guess. Yeah."

"I have to do that because . . . ?"

"*Ne me demandez pas?* How should I know? They got the concierge too."

He cocked his head. "The Downstream is in the international concierge program?"

"I guess. And Sol supposed to have valuated you and send in report. He missed line of dead, so you take paper to Down the River and they send in for you."

85

His mouth dropped open. "Sol was supposed to have finished and returned my evaluation?"

"On the line."

"He was supposed to email it in and missed the deadline, so the university told him to bring it to the Downstream and they would send it in with their evaluation."

"*Exactement.* The packet information waiting for you downstairs. All sealed. Sol toll them you to be there at 2 on the nose."

"Great. Just great."

She kissed his chest. "Too bad we only get the one go 'round right now, eh? But tomorrow you sleep good and we make up for whole summer of no fucking."

He chuckled. "Well, we can get a good start on it, at least." He put a hand behind her head and guided her lips to his and kissed her. "I can't believe we're actually making love. You have no idea how badly I wanted you this whole time."

She shook her head. "No more than me wanting you, Jaz man. . . . If ever you come back to Nola, you come to me?"

Jasper looked at her slyly. "Well that depends. Will Anton still be around?"

She laughed and wiggled her sex against his member. "Only you make Anton disappear into the nothing."

He yawned and stretched. "So Downstream had a concierge apprentice program. It must've been filled before I began to apply." He shook his head and repeated himself. "Downstream had a concierge apprentice. I'll be damned."

"Yeah, most likely," Fleur said. "But today you get showered, get food to eat, go to the Down the River. And you know you name tag?"

"Yes."

"Don't wear you name tag."

The façade of the Downstream Hotel and Resort, white granite formed in traditional French flourishes with darkened glass windows and a revolving door, was an immediate reminder to Jasper of how different his New Orleans apprenticeship was supposed to have been. As he walked into the atrium, gazing up at the openness rising eighteen floors above him, he found himself envying the unknown concierge apprentice who had served this hotel for the summer. There was a solemn silence in the interior of the building and even the air had none of the scents of the French Quarter or the slight mustiness of the *Plaisir*.

As he approached the check-in desk, he pulled the sealed manila envelope from beneath his arm. The uniformed assistant behind the counter, an African-American woman in her forties, looked up at him and smiled.

"How are you, ma'am," he said. "I'm dropping off some papers regarding the concierge apprentice program."

The woman took the packet and gazed at the label on the front that said simply, "Jasper Merritt."

She turned toward a taller man in a suit who stood ten feet away with his back to her. "Mr. Albee," she said, "Mr. Merritt is here."

Without turning, the suited man glanced at his watch. He turned toward Jasper. "Right on time, Mr. Merritt."

He took the envelope and walked around to Jasper's side of the counter. He extended his hand.

"I'm Jeremy Albee. I'm the evening concierge."

Jasper smiled, trying not to overreact. "Mr. Albee." He shook his hand vigorously. "Actually, sir, I am acquainted with the excellent quality of your service."

"You are?"

"Yes. I'm on the desk in the evening at the *Hotela Plaisir*. A week or so ago we had a guest for whom you had rendered service above and beyond the ordinary. . . ." He wanted to explain enough for Albee to grasp whom he was describing without mentioning any specifics. "This guest had initially had been staying at the Downstream, but had to leave unexpectedly. She was extremely grateful for the manner in which you handled the whole affair."

The concierge's eyebrows arched in recognition.

"If I don't miss my guess," Jasper said, "you probably did not receive that praise first hand. Not to speak out of school, but I thought you might like to know your service was appreciated."

Albee smiled. "Thank you, Mr. Merritt. If you wouldn't mind having a seat and hanging onto these documents, I've got to head to a meeting and the right person to handle those will be with you momentarily."

"Certainly."

As Albee disappeared toward the elevators, Jasper took a seat near the check-in counter. He studied the vastness of the hotel's interior. How many rooms did it have, he wondered. Eighteen floors with about twenty rooms to a floor. Some floors would have larger suites and some would have more rooms, but most likely the hotel had more than 350 rooms. How would he have done as an apprentice here, he wondered.

Then he grew curious about the sealed evaluation he held in his hand. What had Sol said about him? It was a miracle the forms had been completed at all. Slowly a new awareness began to emerge for him. The forms had been sent via email and Sol did not use email. Fleur checked his messages every day. So she had printed the forms and asked Sol to complete them, but he had forgotten or procrastinated until . . . Fleur, he realized, had saved him. She had filled out the forms. But what about her poor command of English? She must have used the grammar check and spell check on the computer.

"Thank god," he muttered to himself. "I sure hope she reviewed me as well as she screwed me."

"Mr. Merritt?"

Jasper jumped to his feet. A short woman dressed in a navy suit jacket that matched Albee's had come up to the side of his chair. She held out her hand and they shook.

"My name is Alice Fellows. I'm the concierge."

"Hello, ma'am." He held out the manila envelope. "Here are the documents sent over from the *Plaisir*. We appreciate your taking care of them."

The slightest puzzled expression flashed across her face. "Just hang onto those if you will," she said, "and I'll take you to the person who needs them."

"Of course," he said and followed behind her as she immediately began walking.

Making certain to show no emotion, Jasper wondered how many people he had to go through to drop off some evaluation forms. As regimented and formal as the processes at the Downstream were, however, everyone seemed to know exactly what was expected of him or her. This was the professionalism he had sought and expected when he signed up for the apprentice program.

The elevator rose to the fifth floor, dinged and rolled open swiftly. Wordlessly, Alice Fellows turned down the hallway to the right and walked quickly to a massive, floor to ceiling wooden door that had no nameplate. She entered and held the door open long enough for Jasper to follow. The office they entered was obviously a reception area and the young woman behind the desk only glanced up at the two people as they entered and went back to what she had been working on without speaking.

At the back of the reception room was an equally large wooden door through which Fellows entered without knocking, holding it just long enough for Jasper to follow. The first thing that caught his attention—though he looked only from the corner of his eye—was a huge, perfectly clean glass window that gave a wonderful view of the French Quarter, downtown New Orleans and in the background, the Mississippi River.

Immediately, however, he realized there were three other people in the room. Behind the desk sat a suited, aristocratic-looking man in his 50s who was facing his left and looking at the screen of a laptop. Also standing behind the desk, hands in pockets and facing Jasper, was Jeremy Albee. There was a woman seated on the sofa at the far left of the room. It came to him that he knew her. He faced her for an instant and nodded and she nodded back. It was Lorraine Baxter, the woman who summoned him to her room eight weeks ago to open her bottle of wine and then asked him to make love to her. He realized he should not indicate he knew her unless she expressed that she knew him.

The man behind the desk turned from the computer and stood. He leaned across the desk and extended his hand, which Jasper shook without hesitation.

"Mr. Merritt," the man said, "my name is Arthur Baxter. I'm the General Manager of the Downstream. Please, have a seat." He motioned to a chair just in front of his desk.

"Thank you, sir."

Baxter. This was Lorraine's husband. What was happening? What did this have to do with his liaison with Lorraine? Was his career coming undone before him before it ever began? Jasper felt his face flush.

Fellows took the envelope from Jasper and handed it to Arthur Baxter, who ripped it open without hesitation. He pulled out the contents and spread them on the desk before him. Fellows and Albee stood behind him on either side, silently looking over his shoulder at the evaluation forms.

Something like a fan was spinning inside Jasper's chest. What the hell was going on?

"May I call you Jasper, Mr. Merritt?" Baxter asked without looking up.

"Certainly, sir."

"I believe you've met Ms. Fellows and Mr. Albee."

"Yes, I have had the pleasure."

Baxter looked up at the woman sitting on the sofa. "This is my wife, Lorraine."

Jasper turned to her. "A pleasure, ma'am."

"Nice to meet you," she replied in her silky voice.

Jasper tried not to sigh aloud. What a relief. Baxter didn't know that he already knew Lorraine, that he knew how becoming and desirable she was without any clothes at all and how easily she achieved orgasm when aroused and stimulated.

"As I understand it," Baxter continued, "you have worked this summer in the apprentice concierge program at the *Plaisir*?"

"Yes, sir." He decided not to express the reality that in fact there was no training at the Plaisir and that he in actuality had been the night manager.

"And you are a rising senior at Idaho Tech?"

"Yes, sir. I have a double major in hospitality and business."

Baxter made eye contact with him for the first time, smiling genially. "Well, Jasper, how have you liked New Orleans?"

"Very much, Mr. Baxter. I learned a great deal—well, enough that I could recommend sites and activities for our guests. I learned a lot about the history of Nola and the Quarter."

"Did you tour the area and enjoy the local flavor?"

Jasper nodded. "To the extent I could, sir, given the constraints of my work responsibilities."

"Oh yes. You had the evening shift, 8 p.m. to 8 a.m., Monday through Friday." Baxter tilted his head. "That's sixty hours, son."

"I suppose so. Yes, sir."

"Didn't you complain about that?"

Restraining a smile, Jasper said, "Well no, sir. I think it sort of comes with the territory of being an apprentice, sort of the way medical resident students understand they are going to spend a year or two working sixty hour weeks."

Baxter nodded slowly, looking back to the documents before him.

Was this some sort of evaluation interview that was part of the apprentice program? Was someone besides his supervisor, Sol, supposed to conduct it? Was Sol even now interviewing the Downstream apprentice?

"Did you get along well with the staff?" Baxter asked.

"Oh, yes, sir. The staff is, in many case, quite competent."

Baxter looked up at Jasper with an expression that asked for clarification. "Many cases?"

"If I may elaborate, sir."

"Please do."

"In particular there were co-workers there whose abilities—" He searched for the proper wording. "—exceeded their responsibilities at the *Plaisir*. The head of housekeeping, for instance, has regularly undertaken tasks for the hotel that have helped insure its profitability. If I don't miss my guess, sir, you likely have a large housekeeping staff here at the Downstream. Should you have an opening and extend the opportunity to her, I think you would find quickly that she could rise to be the head of the entire department in short order."

Baxter waited for him to finish speaking and said, "That would be Fleur Printemps."

Jasper tried not to react. "Yes, sir."

Baxter nodded. "And were you not going to mention the head of maintenance, who I understand is also very capable?"

How much did Baxter know, about the hotel and about him? Jasper couldn't decide whether to shut up or to speak more freely.

"I believe you might be referring to Manuel Trevino," Jasper said. "He is a mechanic genius, sir. And has a wonderfully cooperative attitude. I did not mention him to you in that I think he might still be trying to clarify some issues in regard to his green card."

"He's an illegal then," Baxter said matter-of-factly. "Here at the Downstream we've had a fair amount of success in helping people deal with immigration issues."

"Yes, sir."

Baxter tapped his fingers on the spotless desk before him. "You may know, Jasper, that the Downstream also participates in the concierge apprentice program."

"Actually I just found that out today, sir."

"Um hmm. I must say that, in your case, the things your supervisor, Mr. Simon, wrote about you are quite complimentary. He writes that you have 'a gift for service,' 'an intuitive sense of protocol and appropriateness,' 'unflagging enthusiasm,' and 'calm professionalism in the most difficult situations.'"

Fleur had written those things? No. She wouldn't even have known many of the words. Those certainly didn't sound like things Sol would—or could—write either.

"That's very affirming to hear, sir," Jasper said quietly. "Those are the qualities I tried to attain. It's significant to me to know my supervisor thought I had achieved them."

"Yes," Baxter said. "Well, we didn't have such an excellent experience with our apprentice this summer. To be sure, he is a fine fellow who will no doubt find work in the hospitality field, but he did not measure up to our hopes and expectations."

"I'm sorry to hear that, Mr. Baxter."

"Yes, well we were especially disappointed because our intention was to offer our apprentice a permanent position after his graduation. And it didn't work out. So now we find ourselves looking for an exemplary candidate to become a concierge trainee. That's where my lovely wife comes in. You see, Lorraine is an officer for a company that supplies a variety of goods for many of the finer hotels in New Orleans and along the Gulf Coast. She was able to ask many of my colleagues in discrete terms who might be qualified for this position." He stared at Jasper. "And the one person above all who seemed right was you."

Jasper felt his jaw drop. He had no idea how to respond.

"Now that you've completed your apprenticeship, Jasper, do you think you'd be open to a position at the Downstream after you graduate?"

He straightened in his chair. He was wildly thrilled and at the same time felt totally like a fraud.

"Uh, sir. . . ."

"Yes?"

"I would jump in the Mississippi for a chance to work here, Mr. Baxter. However I need to be frank with you, sir." How could he say it? "I fear the quality of the training your apprentice received—whether he failed you or not—was quite superior to the quality of the training I received."

"Yes. We are absolutely aware of that, Jasper. Would you be open to the offer of a position after your graduation?"

"Yes, sir. I certainly would, sir."

"I'm pleased to hear that, son." Baxter leaned back in his chair.

There was motion on the couch to his left. Lorraine shifted and stood and for the first time she spoke.

"Excuse me, folks," she said. "I need to get back to my real job. Will you be home on time tonight, Arthur?"

"Give me until 6."

"See you then. Congratulation, Mr. Merritt."

"Uh, yes, ma'am. And thank you so much for your research."

"To give you an idea of what happens next," Baxter said, as Lorraine walked from the office, "we already have all your contact information. When you get back to Idaho, you'll receive documents to complete and return to us. We would like you onsite by June 1 of next year."

"Yes, sir."

"We will be sending you a small stipend in mid-May to help with your relocation expenses. We start our concierge trainees at $38,000 plus benefits: health and life insurance, 401K and business expenses. This is not a great starting salary because, upon your arrival, we will begin a tuition fund for you. We've found that a concierge benefits greatly from having an MBA. So after you complete your first year with us, we'll encourage you to find an appropriate program and we'll pay for you to complete it. When you do, your salary will be increased commensurate with your credentials."

The fan was turning inside his chest again. Only this time the thrill was one of joy.

"Yes, sir. Excellent."

"You will have questions." He looked at Fellows, who handed her card to Jasper. "Whatever you want to know, just contact Ms. Fellows."

Baxter stood. And Jasper stood.

"Welcome aboard, Jasper. We're glad you'll be part of the Downstream."

"Thank you so much, sir. You will not regret this decision. I'm

. . . grateful beyond words."

"You're welcome." He nodded toward the door. "And you can find your way out?"

"Yes, sir."

Jasper tried to walk as normally as possible and not run into the furniture or doorframe as he left the room and gingerly closed the door.

The assistant looked up from her computer and smiled at him. "My name is Natalie, Jasper. Welcome to the Downstream."

"Thank you, ma'am. I need to go find a place where I can scream right now."

Smiling, she looked back down.

Jasper closed the door to the outer office and scanned the hallway. He started toward the stairwell.

"Hey." It was Lorraine's voice. She had been leaning against the carpeted wall of the outer office. "You don't have to use the stairs. You can trust the elevators here at the Downstream. Come on."

She walked with him to the elevator and pressed the call button. She glanced at him as he stood beside her silently.

"So what do you think?" she asked.

"I'm just waiting for my heart to start beating again. I know that something amazingly wonderful and good just happened. I'm still trying to process it."

Lorraine shrugged. "It's nothing more than you earned and deserve, Jasper."

The elevator door rolled open and they stepped inside. Lorraine pushed a button and the doors closed.

"I can't get over that evaluation," he said. "I thought at first that Flo had written it, but there's no way. And there's no way that Sol could have said those things."

The woman smiled. "Maybe they had some help."

He turned to her. "You did it! You filled out my evaluation."

"Well, let's say I took Flo aside a few days ago and together we filled it out. Regardless of who did it, everything we said was absolutely accurate. You're going to be an outstanding employee and concierge."

". . . Are we going up?"

"Yes," she said. "Don't you want to see the view from the eighteenth floor?"

"Sure."

In a moment there was a ding and the door rolled open to a hallway. Lorraine took his hand and led him down the hall to a door that, like the general manager's office, had no sign or number. She ran a card through the mechanism and a green light blinked. She opened the door and, still holding his hand, took him into a grand suite dominated by floor to ceiling windows with a view of the entire city and winding river. In the center of the room was a perfectly round bed and directly above the bed on the ceiling was a perfectly round mirror.

"What room is this?"

"When I travel, my company books rooms for stays. They ask no questions about my accommodations. This is one of the rooms I like to stay in at the Downstream."

"Wow. So this is not, you know, Mr. Baxter's . . ."

She slipped out of her high heels. "Mr. Baxter has no idea I book this room." She took his hand and guided him to the window and they stood looking out over the breathtaking view.

She turned to him. "Well, Jasper, aren't you going to show me your appreciation?"

Also by Stone Cruz from Weeping Rose Books and Indigo Sea Press:

Lisa Newsome, a certified nursing assistant, is trying to rebuild her life after a brutal divorce. Struggling to make ends meet as she completes her RN training, she is summoned to serve three days as a home health care nurse for a rodeo cowboy, LT Tolliver, who has been brutalized in lots of other ways. It turns out that each needs the healing the other has to offer—and a chance to get **Back in the Saddle**.

Pet, the Teacher, had long since given up on anything like romance in her life. Then came the day when a stranger entered the elementary classroom behind her, startling her and beginning a chain of events that would utterly destroy her expectations and ignite within her a passion she never knew was possible.